LIL MAMA: TALES FROM THE HOOD 2

WRITTEN BY:

MS. STREET CRED

Lil Mama: Tales From The Hood 2

Copyright © 2018 by Ms. Street Cred

All rights reserved.

Published in the United States of America.

Published by Twyla T. Presents, LLC.

Dedication

"How many caskets can we witness

Before we see it's hard to live

This life without God, so we must ask forgiveness"

-Tupac

Acknowledgements

First and foremost I'd like to give all praises to the Lord above for blessing me with the talent to be able to put words together. This is my third book and a great way to kickoff 2019. Writing this duology has been such a crazy experience yet I have grown not only as a writer but as a person. TTP has been the foundation I needed to feel like I was apart of something bigger than myself. Twyla T has been instrumental in my progress as a writer.

To my silent and vocal supporters I appreciate and love you all. It is because of ya'll I fight and push to produce quality work. To the growing readers you guys rock! If it was not for your love of reading there would be no me. I am grateful for every person who has joined me on this wild journey and I hope you guys buckle up because it only gets wilder. My Angel mother saw something in me as a child and fueled the fire in me then. While she may not be here with me I know she is looking down on me proud. I hope you guys are ready because 2019 is going to be crazy!

--M$C

Chapter 1

|Dasiah|

We found prime parking right up front when we got to the hospital. As we made our way inside, I waved at the same security guard that I'd seen every time I'd been back since leaving Jayceon here. As we made our way up on the elevator to the NICU, I couldn't wait to see my son, talk to the doctors on what his prognosis was, and how much recovery he would need before I could finally take him home. As the doors to the elevator opened, there was a loud blaring alarm going off. I saw NICU nurses and doctors sprinting down the hall towards the direction we're headed. I looked down the hall and saw someone standing near the entry of my son's room. From just the back of him, I knew who it was. Jordan was standing there with his hands on his head, pacing. I felt my heart stop. And looking over at the man standing beside me, I saw Khalil tense up like a rabid animal, ready to attack his prey. My steps quicken once I realized it was indeed my son's room that everyone was rushing to. Khalil's chest was puffed out as we got closer to Jayceon's room. In a split second, Lil took off full speed, charging towards Jordan. I couldn't stop him even if I wanted to. He had Jordan pinned up on the wall by now with his forearm under his neck, restricting his air.

"What yo pussy ass doing here nigga? Haven't you done enough to this girl?" Lil snarled at him.

Jordan visibly looked defeated, and even though I wasn't ready to face him, right now wasn't the time or place for all of this. Visitors and nurses were now witnessing the debacle, and I was feeling quite embarrassed. I grabbed Lil by his shoulder and reasoned with him.

"Lil right now ain't the time. I know how you feel and what you said, but we will have to handle this another time." I said as I saw hospital security coming towards us.

He must of seen them coming too because he released his hold and shoved Jordan one last time before backing away from him and letting out a loud sigh. I knew what he wanted to do. I'm sure Jordan knew too, but right now, my attention needed to be on my son. I was up on the glass outside his room, watching his little body shake uncontrollably. I couldn't bare to watch as my son fought helplessly. I backed away from the window and started to sob. I felt Khalil come up from behind me as I fell back into his arms and cried. The security guards were about to say something, but given the circumstances, neither of them spoke; instead, they posted up further down the hall to keep an eye on things. I could see doctors and nurses swapping medical tools and doing everything to save him. From where I stood, I could see he had stopped shaking. I saw a few of them drop their heads and shake them before they started clearing out of the room one by one. A robust looking nurse came from the nurse's station. I had never met her before. She instructed us that there was a private waiting room where the hospital Chaplin and Dr. Patel would be there shortly to speak with me. No matter how much I wanted to make my feet move, they just would not.

"What y'all need the fuckin' Chaplin for?" I heard Lil question the nurse.

"Sir that is something the doctor will discuss with you guys in a more private setting." She said before walking us to the private area and leaving us there. Jordan came slithering in a few moments later. Just the sight of him made me explode.

"Why the fuck you here?!!" I screamed at the top of my lungs. It took everything in me not to go up in that nigga shit. I was heated.

Khalil wasn't trying to stop me either. Before I lost all senses and ran down on his ass, the door to the waiting area opened and Dr. Patel as well as the Chaplin came in. They both wore melancholy expressions on their faces. The tension between Lil, Jordan, and I was thick but not as thick as it was about to be.

"Is it ok if we discuss this in front of these two Ms. Nguyen?" I shook my head yes as I braced myself for what Dr. Patel was about to say.

"After extensive monitoring and just allowing Jayceon's body to try and develop on its own, he unfortunately went into cardiac arrest. And since he is a preterm birth, we suspect that those issues along with other factors ultimately played a role in the death of your son Ms. Nguyen." Dr. Patel spoke tenderly.

Everything started spinning around me. I heard the doctor clear as day, but nothing or no one was about to tell me my son was gone. I had carried him. I could hear the Chaplin reciting the serenity prayer as Jordan all but collapsed on the floor. I couldn't understand why he was breaking down. He was the fucking reason our son had been in here in the first place. Without logically thinking and my common sense all but gone, I rushed him as he sat on the ground where he had collapsed. I went Super Saiyan on this nigga. I made every lick connect. By now, Khalil and Dr. Patel were pulling me off this nigga's ass. He just sat there and cried harder.

I was livid! I could feel my feet leaving the ground as I broke down completely. The last thing I remember seeing was security escorting Jordan out.

|Jordan|

I was sitting in my car, still crying from the news that my son was dead. This was all my fault; I couldn't deny that. I wasn't surprised to see Dasiah with that street thug. I knew my fuck up would just draw them closer together. I felt shitty that the first time I ever laid eyes on my son was the last time. I had put my own son at risk. I dreaded calling my mother and informing her of what had happened. The whole time I was home, she kept asking about Dasiah and the baby. What was I suppose to say now? I couldn't keep up the lie anymore. I looked at my tear stained face in the rearview mirror. I looked horrible but I felt worse.

I inadvertently killed my own son and no one could tell me otherwise. Had I not been in my feeling about a stupid ass text message, I wouldn't be here right now, coping with the loss of him. I wanted to drive anywhere but back to Daylen's. I knew he would take this news with a jovial approach, and this wasn't something to be happy about or joke about. I hadn't been ready to see Dasiah with Khalil, and when he ran up on me, I kinda panicked. I was a big bad wolf in front of females, but in front of another man, I would bitch up. I wasn't bred for street shit, but I knew what I had done had earned me a grade A ass whoopin' courtesy of Khalil. When Dasiah fired off on me, that really hurt me to see her like that. I never meant to hurt her. She didn't deserve what I had done to her, and I would forever beat myself up over this.

After thirty minutes of sulking in my car, I finally started it and drove off, not heading anywhere in particular but definitely not headed back to Daylen's. I would rather not be around him as I mourned my son. I pulled into the same McDonald's parking lot I had came to a few weeks prior and simply parked. I wasn't hungry. I wasn't thirsty. I was simply defeated. Coming back here was suppose to clear the air not make it thicker. I felt like I was suffocating, but by my own hands. I was sitting in my car with my head practically glued to the headrest as today's events played over and over again in my head. When she walked out of the restaurant to a beat up Cadillac that was parked, I had no intentions of speaking to her. I wanted to sit here in my shit and continue to stew, but seeing her again brought some type of sunshine to my life. I don't know how I ended up out the car and walking over to her car. But after knocking on her window and nearly startling the girl, she apprehensively rolled her window down. I was met with her beautiful smile.

"Hi, can I help you?" she asked, fumbling with her seatbelt.

"Actually I was wondering if I could take you out sometime?" I asked her with the best smile I could muster. I know it was bold and brazen for me to approach her, but given everything I had going on, I needed something new and exciting in my life. Dasiah was clearly about to fall back into the arms of a street thug, and I had nothing or no one to call my own. I watched as she ripped a piece of paper she had found in her car and then found a pen and scribbled something on it.

"Well, here's my name and number. If I ain't the one, lose it, if I am, use it." She said before giving me a wink and putting her car in reverse. She gave me a quick wave before pulling out of the parking lot, leaving me staring at her name and number. Candice…. but wait! Her name tag said Shayna that day I saw her.

|Daniya|

Glee had been knocking me down anytime and anywhere between us getting money, and I didn't mind at all. I was starting to smell myself. If I had known this was what it was like getting dick, I probably would have been fuckin'. We had been going at it for days since that initial time. I was still careful though, making sure he always had a rubber. He was good about having some, given we had been going at it like we were rabbits with no signs of slowing down. I craved his touch and the way his dick felt in me, and if it wasn't for both of our phones ringing about money, I would never leave his spot for anything. I was getting everything and more courtesy of Glee.

I was sitting at the trap finishing up a couple plays while Glee was busy whoopin' Tez's ass in Madden '01. I literally couldn't tell anyone that asked the last time I had been to my God mom's. She knew that I was breathing and that's all she cared about. I just knew that if things didn't pan out with Glee that I had a bed at her place, no questions asked. I'm sure my mother was up in heaven shaking her head at my antics and probably cursing my God mom out for letting me do whatever. But only God could judge me and that's how I saw life. No one could talk down on what I had going on because only God had that final say so.

I was cutting up smaller squares off the cooked crack that I had done earlier in the day. It had finally dried and was about to be hitting buddies' hands within the hour. I used a razor blade to get my squares the right size. Making sure not to chip or crack it because that would be a major foul, and I'd be missing out on money for a broken piece. I got each little piece in the clear baggies and snapped them close. I knew we would be headed north later, and I wanted party favors, just in case we ran into people that wanted to have a lil fun. Glee and Tez had been taking me to these drug induced parties, where I could mingle and make a decent amount of money in one night. Them shits had become addicting and I was always looking forward to going to one. Glee and I would almost always sell out and then we'd go sit in his car and smoke several blunts back to back before I'd suck him up from the passenger's seat and finish him off once we got home.

As I finished up my task, a message alert stops me from finishing. I glance down at my phone and my eyes swell with tears. I slam my fist down angrily on the table as the tears started to sting my eyes. I know I startled the guys because before, I could hear the games noise but right now, there was nothing registering. Seconds later, I lost it! My arms flailed about like Tre in *"Boyz N The Hood"* after he got back to Brandi's house after he and Ricky were harassed by the cops. I hadn't realized that I was now fighting Glee as he attempted to calm me down.

"Why my nephew?" I sobbed as tears and snot met above my lip, making probably the nastiest sight for anyone. I could care less about how my face looked or what was on it. I was pissed Jordan's faggot ass had succeeded in bringing more pain to my sister's life, and now I was going to make his ass pay.

"Niya, I'm so sorry." Glee comforted me.

I instantly felt a headache come on.

My heart ached for my sister. After all she had endured, she was still being slighted by God.

****

"Lil mama you gotta eat something." Glee said from the driver's seat as he smashed his Checker's burger and large fry. We had just left Checker's and headed back east on I-4 with our sights on Daytona. We had about another hour before we reached there. Glee had gotten hungry and pretty much detoured off the interstate due to the food signs near the exit. He knows I high-key like Checker's and so does he, so it was a no brainer where he was going. I didn't even have to tell him my order, and while I wanted the Big

Buford and the fries that accompanied it, I didn't have an appetite. I was still trying to wrap my head around my nephew's death. Dasiah texting me that really fucked up my day.

I was due to make my rounds at a few parties tonight, and I'd be missing hella money, but Jayceon's death trumped money any day. I was so confused as to what could have happened that fast. Dasiah told me recently that he was getting better, but now, we would be laying him to rest. I would never see him grow up; he never even met me.

I was so down about the shit, I never answered Glee. I just looked out the window in my own world. Seconds later, I could hear Pastor Troy's voice blare out of the car speakers as *"No Mo Play in G.A."* played. He been playing the hell out of this damn CD and I was about over Pastor damn Troy, but I started finding myself rapping to some of the lyrics. I couldn't wait till I had saved enough money to get a car. I had my eyes on a brand new '01 Altima but with a lot of custom features. I was nowhere close to having the funds, but with three hundred already saved, it might not have been much to someone else but it meant everything to me. I hadn't even mentioned it to Glee. I zoned out looking out the window, letting my thoughts take over.

After another hour and one bathroom break, we pulled up to my sister's apartment complex. I hadn't been back here since the incident that started the omen on my sister and nephew. I instantly got mad thinking back to that day. I stepped out the car as the late November weather was just right. Glee grabbed our bags, and I led him upstairs to my sister's apartment. Before I could knock, the door opened and we were greeted by Lil.

"Wassup y'all?" he said, hugging me and dapping Glee up before moving to the side to let us in.

Walking back in here, the space felt different, like there was a new energy here. Dasiah was sitting on the couch, rolling up. Her eyes were already naturally chinky, but they looked damn near closed. I had never known my sister to smoke, but seeing her high as a giraffe's pussy had lifted my spirits a bit.

"Baby sister!" She exclaimed, sealing the end of the blunt before sitting it on the table, jumping up off the couch, and giving me a tight hug. I hugged her back with just as much intensity. I wanted my sister to know I was there for her. While I couldn't understand her pain, I knew she forged a bond with Jayceon before she ever laid eyes on him.

We finally let one another go as she walked back over to her spot on the couch and plopped down. She immediately picked up the blunt she had just rolled and sparked it. Khalil took a seat right next to her, rubbing her thigh affectionately when he sat down. I had seen the exchange and would make it my business to ask Dasiah about it because I knew their history all too well.

Glee sat down on the loveseat as I made my way over to the single seat that the modern day rocker provided. Glee gave me a look before chuckling to himself and pulling a pre-rolled El out and sparking it. I followed suit with my own pre-rolled blunt that was stuffed with the finest kush anyone could get their hands on. With three blunts in rotation and Lil twisting up a forth, we all enjoyed the vibe and our smoke session.

|Alani|

"Ugh! Why did my fuckin' period have to come on?" I yelled while on the toilet, looking at the bloody piece of tissue. I had planned on getting my ass ate and a few more fetish type things by this nigga named Malcolm, but everybody that knew him called him Mack. I used to mess with him a couple years ago when I turned fourteen, but once he found out how old I was, he stopped fucking with me. I mean his ass was all of twenty one at the time, but his ass turned me out to sex. My high drive and my nympho tendencies that I had now were all thanks to Mack, and when I ran into him last night at the corner store, my lil pussy did a cartwheel and a somersault just at the sight of him.

Mack was caked up and had the looks to match. He stood at six one, was slim, and had skin the color of onyx. If he had any tattoos, you would have to hold a light up to him to see them. He was always dressed in the latest shit. The nigga stayed clean, but his dick was community dick for sure. He had enough money to run several households and wasn't afraid to put a baby in any bitch that he saw fit to paint her walls. I knew he had five kids, but word on the streets was that there were really eight with a possible on the way. I could care less about any of the baby nonsense. I was strictly trying to get my five minutes to shine, so he could break me off some bread and some dick.

Now here I was about to miss out on a dick I hadn't had in over two years. I retrieved a tampon out of the drawer next to the toilet and finished preparing myself for a few days of mood swings and chocolate binges. When I got back in my room, I crawled right back in bed. I had been in it all day, trying to ignore the intense pains in my abdomen and lower region, but I couldn't stop them if I tried. I retrieved my phone from under the covers before shooting Mack a text, asking for a rain check. He texted back immediately, letting me know that was fine because something had come up for him anyways. I texted him for a little while longer before dozing back off to sleep with hopes these cramps would be gone.

****

"You ain't never gone stop fucking for money hoe!"

I jumped up out of my sleep to the never ending arguing between my mama and her boyfriend. I wish that I had the money to just leave this place. Sadly, I didn't know when I'd ever have the funds to get out of this city. Suddenly, there was a loud crash followed by the sounds of glass shattering and then you could hear the door slamming. I didn't want to get up to see what was going on, but I knew I had to. So many nights Mike had beaten the dog shit out of my mother and many nights my brother and I would have to nurse her wounds. The shit got tiresome and I was at my wits ends with their continuous bullshit; it was a never ending cycle. I made my way to where most of their fights began and ended, the living room. My mama was sitting on the floor near a pile of glass.

"Lani gone back to bed girl, I got this."

She said without looking up at me. It was either because she had a new black eye or that she too was tired of seeing herself being abused. Yet every time she thought to leave, Mike would come home with the wining and dining bullshit he pulled and my mama would be right back in that nigga's clutches. I disregarded my mother's request, going to the kitchen to retrieve the broom and dustpan and a pack of frozen peas. I walked over to where she was and helped her up before handing her the frozen vegetables for her eye. She took a seat on the dingy worn out couch that had occupied our living room since we moved into this house and sparked up a 305.

I swept up the broken glass from the lamp that had fallen due to their fight and collected all the broken pieces and took them outside to the dumpster. When I walked back in, my mama had retreated to her bedroom, probably waiting for Mike to return. I went back to my room, in hopes that I could rest. One thing I missed about Niya was that when shit like this went on, I could always call her to get away if just for a few hours. I quickly shook the good thoughts of my once best friend out of my head and thought about mine and Keno's plan to get back at all they asses. They would regret the day they tried us.

Chapter 2

|Daylen|

Life was feeling so perfect right now. Having Jordan to myself with that big headed half Asian bitch out of the picture was everything to me. I was currently in the kitchen whipping up Jordan's favorite meal, enchiladas and black beans and rice. I knew my way around the kitchen thanks to my granny, and I took pride in being able to cook. It was one of my many talents that I used to keep my man happy. I had planned a quiet night at home with no added distractions from school or anyone. I was going to suck the living soul out of Jordan and put him in a deep sleep. I know he had been contemplating going down to the hospital to see his son, but he had never truly decided. He had been gone all day and hadn't responded to any of my text messages, but I was trying to not get mad. I knew it was over between him and Dasiah, and by now, the entire campus knew what had happened. I even added to the gossip by telling what I had heard, but I knew it was all factual information that I was helping to spread. I didn't give a fuck that I was messy or that I was painting my man in a bad light. I wanted the entire student body to know that Dasiah and Jordan were over. They had been a rememberable couple at Cookman and now everyone knew that their seemingly perfect relationship was anything but.

As I spread the taco sauce over the enchiladas, I stuck them back in the oven for a bit, hoping they would turn out how he liked. The clock on the stove read seven forty five and I still hadn't gotten a text back. I was growing annoyed, but I didn't want to irritate Jordan with my constant texting, so I decided to do a pick me up line of coke to take the edge off, waiting for my man to return home. I wasn't a frequent user, but it definitely helped those nights I was up studying and needed to push through. Right now, I just wanted to get my mind off where Jordan was and what he was doing. The oven timer went off, letting me know the food was done. I retrieved the Mexican favorite out of the oven and covered it with foil before turning off the oven and retrieving the Sparkling Verdi wine out of the freezer. I popped the top, pouring damn near the whole bottle in the goblet that I had grabbed out of the dish drainer. I was trying to relax my nerves; the line I had done minutes ago needed a little bit of liquor courage to get the full effects. I put on my R&B mixed CD that I had got from the local hair store and funked out to Mary J Blige.

****

Two bottles of Verdi later and three hours with the same CD on repeat had me feeling emotional and tipsy all at the same time. I had since begun blowing Jordan's phone up and now it was going straight to voicemail. I was becoming angrier by the minute. I threw my Razr on the couch and plopped down before doing another line of coke. I wiped the residue from my nose and flicked on the TV. There was nothing on at ten at night, and I started feeling my heart racing. Was Jordan with Dasiah? Was he with another man? My thoughts were running amuck, and I started to think irrational. I was feeling restless and more agitated as ten o'clock turned into twelve a.m. Jordan still wasn't back, and I found myself having unnatural thoughts. I retrieved my phone and attempted for the hundredth time to reach Jordan. When I heard the automated voice for his voicemail pick up once again, I lost it. I knocked my collection of JET magazines off the table, turned up the couches, pushed over my CD tower, and punched the biggest hole in the wall. I was on a rampage and Jordan was the cause of it all.

How could he just ignore me like he was doing? Had I not been playing my role? I looked down at my now bleeding and swollen hand and went in my bathroom to search the medicine cabinet for anything to help aid in stopping the bleeding. I looked at myself briefly as I retrieved the small first aid kit out of the cabinet. My eyes had dark circles underneath and my nose was running. I sucked the snot back up before wiping my nose with the back of my uninjured hand. I opened the kit and grabbed a roll of gauze wraps and a tube of Neosporin. I slid down the wall of the bathroom and attempted to doctor on myself. The hand I had injured was my dominant hand so trying to apply the ointment and wrap it myself was a huge task. After ten minutes of wrapping and unwrapping my hand, I finally felt secure in the job I had done and stumbled out of the bathroom and into the room I had been sharing with the man I thought loved me. I was going to try and rest but with no correspondence from Jordan, that was going to be a hard task.

|Keno|

Word on the street was that nigga Khalil was ducked off somewhere in Daytona with that pretty bitch Dasiah. I should have dropped my dope dick in her when I had the chance. Had my nigga Chauncey stuck with my plan all those years ago, lil Mulan would have easily been my lady. I was cruising the streets late night, possibly looking for something to get into. Ever since a nigga got out of jail, I couldn't seem to catch none of my old hoes. Most of them bitches had moved on with a nigga a lil higher up on the totem pole than me or they asses knew that my temper was way worse than before and knew my beatings would be even more lethal. I took a slow drag off the el po I had rolled. It didn't take much for me to get high right now since I hadn't been out even a month yet. I did my time, thinking about the day that I'd be able to catch up with Khalil and that group of bitch ass niggas he ran with. I had been driving by where they hung out at the last few nights because I couldn't believe that nigga had really been gone out the city this long. Them niggas he ran with were dumb as fuck. I could have bodied half his niggas with their non-observant asses.

Lil cuz was going to help me with my plan. While she was family, her ass was mad over some little shit if you asked me, but I had to respect lil cuz's mind because she felt disrespected. I could only help her while she helped me. Our plan would go down in two weeks if what the baser who I had hitting their trap up told me right. That nigga Glee was planning a birthday party for the lil bitch Daniya and lil cuz was going to get her get back while putting me in the right position to get mine. Somebody's mama was going to be in all black and I preferred it be Khalil's; but I was all for making a statement with whomever was in my visual. I started to get hungry and the only place that was still open at this time of the night was Gyros. I hit a u-turn on Ninth Street and headed towards Sixteenth Street. I knew Gyros was probably swangin' and that most of the people leaving the club would be there, trying to soak up all that liquor. When I pulled into the parking lot to the popular late night food spot, it was packed as predicted. There was no drive thru, so I was going to have to go in and order and hoped to grab a couple bitches' numbers while I was in there too. I grabbed the first spot that came available and hopped out. I observed niggas parking lot pimpin' while they waited for their food, and if I wasn't hungry, I probably would have posted up too, trying to catch a nice piece of ass coming out. Hell who said I still wouldn't once I smashed this food?

After sliding the cashier money for my twenty wings and fries, I slid in one of the booths and focused on the small TV up in the corner of the restaurant. There wasn't shit on worth watching, but it was worth watching long enough to get my food. Suddenly, a group of four young broads walked in; one was louder than all of her friends, but she caught my eye instantly. I eavesdropped on their conversation as they waited in line to order their food.

"Bitch Devaughn gone fuck yo ass up." One of the girls said to the louder girl.

"Fuck him! He better be worried about bringing my damn baby some diapers... his bitch ass already ain't paying child support." The girl responded as she fished out a tube of lip gloss from her purse.

She looked up at me and our eyes locked. She gave me a lil sly smile. I loved me a lil hoodrat bitch and whoever this nigga they was talking about was, he was about to be mad at a nigga 'cause I was about to shoot my shot.

I watched her cute ass apply the lip gloss on her lips, just observing her rub her lips together had me imagining what it would be like for her plump juicy lips to be wrapped around my dick. I felt my soldier rising to attention as I thought about bending her lil thick ass over. My thoughts were interrupted by one of her friends talking real loud, grabbing everyone in the restaurants attention.

"Ain't that Zeke out there in that big eyed bitch Patrice's face?" An equally good looking girl said.

"Shad don't go out there causing no scene." A soft spoken girl piped up and said.

"Nah fuck all dat! Bitch let's go grease this bitch ass." The girl I had my eyes on instigated.

"See Stasi... that's why this bitch always getting in fights 'cause of bitches like you hyping her ass up." The equally good looking girl said.

I glanced outside myself, observing a nigga standing outside a purple and gold Monte Carlo, clearly entertaining another bitch.

The cashier got my attention long enough to tell me my food was up. As I walked over to the counter to grab my order, the loud mouth girl looked my way one more time before licking her lips. I definitely wanted to see what that mouth was about. I walked past them and then outside back to my car. I retrieved a piece of old receipt paper and found a pen and scribbled down my info before jogging back inside. By now, the loud mouth one was at the counter, and I politely pushed up next to her.

"Here sexy, give me a call sometime." I said, flashing my imperfect smile at her. She smiled back at me before taking the piece of paper and sliding it in her purse. As I left out, I could hear one of her friends say,

"Bitch... Dee gone fuck you up."

The other girl, whose man I assumed was outside disrespecting her, was now sitting on the hood of the Monte Carlo, talking cash shit to the nigga. I chuckled before hopping in my own ride to peel off. I was really hoping the lil sexy bitch used the number. I could only promise her a few unforgettable nights, but they would be well worth it. I headed back cross Thirty Fourth to my mom's crib to smash this food.

|Glee|

We had gotten to Dasiah's apartment a little after nine last night, and after several blunts to the face, Niya and I crashed in the room almost immediately after the last blunt was put out. Out of respect for Dasiah and my nigga Lil, I tried my hardest not to fuck the shit out of Daniya. While we weren't still officially together, she was mine. She might not had of known but my dick, my mouth, and my heart knew she belonged to me. I tried not to put my hands on her all night, but she kept pushing her ass up against me, trying to tempt me. What was a young nigga suppose to do? I felt my nature rising, so I slid out of the bed from next to my future everything. Yes, Niya had my nose wide the fuck open and unlike any other female I had dealt with, she was the most chill and understanding out of all of them. She made a nigga wanna be around her cute ass every day. Her sixteenth birthday was right around the corner, and I had planned a party she wouldn't forget. I just hadn't factored in her sister's baby passing; now my lil boo was all in her feelings and the situation had all of us heated. Dasiah got twisted last night after we eventually got settled in, and I knew it was her way of coping with the loss of her son.

I looked back at Daniya sleeping before creeping out the bedroom into the hall. I could see the light from the TV in the living room but couldn't hear any sounds. I knew Khalil was up, sitting there in silence, probably not even watching the TV. I detoured to the bathroom before checking on my dawg. I wanted to jack off so bad, but my conscious wouldn't allow me to. I just wasn't into beating off other than at my own spot. Call me weird but I was never going to be that horny out in public. I drained my dragon after downing a few shots last night with Khalil and Dasiah. I had been lit myself. Niya rarely drank; she mostly babysat drinks and I liked that she wasn't a big drinker. Once I finished pissin', I washed my hands with the cucumber melon scented hand soap and rinsed them. I shook the excess water off my hands and flicked the light off, heading towards the illumination coming from the end of the hall. When I made it to the end of the hallway, I saw my boy rolling up while two hippos fought on Animal Planet on TV.

"Wassup bro? Can't sleep?" I inquired before taking a seat on the other end of the sofa.

"Shit dawg, you know how I be." Lil said, sealing the el po he just rolled up before grabbing the BIC lighter off the coffee table in front of him and sparking up the potent blend of white widow and bubble gum kush.

I knew my dawg had a lot on his mind and being here with Dasiah was his main focus. I knew hearing the news that Keno was out and looking to settle his beef weighed heavy on my nigga, and regardless if he was in the Da Burg or not, that nigga Keno could get his issue from any one of us. He just needed to do like a frog and leap.

"My nigga, we gotta get rid of that nigga Keno." Khalil spoke as he exhaled smoke out of his nose.

"Hell yeah! Ion want that nigga to get too comfortable with being out in these streets. He probably think shit sweet for him or something." I replied, taking the blunt out of Lil's hand.

"Waiting till that nigga fuck up on his own, only for him to end up back in jail just ain't what I want for that nigga... he gotta die. He been talking too much shit even from jail." Lil said.

Him saying that reminded me that we had received several bullshit ass threats and lil niggas coming home telling us how that pussy ass nigga had been running his mouth the whole time about us. You would have thought that nigga would have used his time wisely, but no! He was too caught up with what me and my niggas was doing.

"Yeah we gone have to handle that nigga fosho." I said, passing the joint back to one of my longest friends.

When I met Khalil, I ain't have shit and I ain't want shit outta life. Now, a young nigga had the drive and mind to be the boss that my nigga Khalil told me I was destined to be. And soon, this King would have a Queen to help run my growing street empire. I couldn't shake Daniya; to me, she was ideal. She wasn't green to the life I led and lil mama was a rider. I had to lock her down asap, and I knew just how I was going to do it.

"So what's going on with you and Niya?" Lil said, exhaling smoke.

" Shiiiid bro... I really like her." I answered honestly.

"Well if you serious about her bro, make sure you all in. Niya is good peoples." Lil said, passing the blunt back my way.

"Hell yeah she is! I love her vibe bro. She make a nigga wanna settle down." I said, thinking more and more about when she's officially mine.

"I just want both of y'all happy, and I want to make sure we all eating good."

"Bro, I am happy. She makes me more happier than I ever been. You remember how fucked up my heart and mind were when I was her age? I was a fucking menace bro." I said, shaking my head at what my attitude use to be like.

I had been tossed into a fucked up situation from birth, yet here I was still going on in life. If it wasn't for my dawg right here, I'd probably be dead or most likely in prison. I owed this nigga my life. The first shorty that I had was getting this nigga as they God daddy and that was a promise. I wouldn't trust my seeds with anybody else. I was nineteen going on twenty in a few months, and I wanted to be settled by the time I was Lil's age.

"Nigga now you know I remember what a fucking terror yo ass was at thirteen, fourteen. Niggas older than me would steer clear of yo crazy ass." Lil said, chuckling.

" Man I wasn't that bad." I said, laughing.

"You think Dasiah and I would work out again?" Lil asked.

Knowing Dasiah and Khalil's history, it was like they were meant to be. Had it not been for Ms. Kandi's mean ass, they probably would have still been together, and we wouldn't be here getting ready to bury a baby. I wanted to answer my dawg's question without making him feel some type of way, but I also had to remind the nigga that he was the reason why they hadn't in the first place.

"Bro in all honesty, you know you're the reason y'all broke up in the first place." I said matter factly.

"Yeah nigga... I know." Lil retorted, letting out a sigh.

"Y'all been spending all this time together and done fucked around and fell back in love." I joked.

"Shit! I ain't never fell out of love with her... to keep it all the way real. I just let my animosity towards her moms and what she made shorty do to my seed that I selfishly pushed my baby away man. Now look at this shit. She traumatized from some shit she should have never been in. That poindexter ass nigga wasn't even Daish speed, yet I let her go, and now she done lost her son. Shit all bad bro." Lil ranted as he rubbed his face with his hand.

I could tell my dawg was frustrated and conflicted. Everybody who knew him and Dasiah had full knowledge of their hood love story. They were supposed to have a couple kids by now. When I was a jit hangin' around the crew, they would always joke with this nigga about how Daish would get this nigga to move out the hood one day. And he knew it too; he would never argue, just simply laugh. Everybody knew what it was, but with life's current events, I personally wouldn't want to insert myself into something so delicate, but this my was nigga's first love. They had real deal history. I could understand if he wanted his old thang back.

"Bro, do what makes you happy. Trust and believe when the moment is right, I'm snatching Niya's lil ass up." I boast proudly.

"You really like her huh man?" Lil was studying my face but with admiration.

"Yeah man, I could see us together for a while." I said.

"Man I wouldn't want her to be with anybody else. I'm sure Daish wouldn't mind having you as her brother." Khalil joked.

"Shiiid... I wouldn't mind having her as a sister." I said back with a laugh.

We smoked another blunt and spent the rest of the early morning talking about how we should handle Keno.

|Jordan|

When I walked into Daylen's apartment, I wasn't expecting it to be turnt upside down. I thought for sure he was in trouble, but upon further inspection, I knew otherwise. I was quite aware of the lil spider monkey on Daylen's back. He loved to snort a couple lines before he studied or before a test, but whatever he had done tonight had clearly sent him over the edge. I had stayed out late on purpose because mentally, I couldn't process the death of my son. Yes, I was the reason he was in the hospital, but I never had intentions of causing deadly harm to him. I knew Daylen like I knew the back of my hands. He would bask in the knowledge that Dasiah was going through something so traumatic. He wouldn't care that she had moved on. Whether it be true or not, I knew she wasn't going to ever come back to me, and no matter how much I wanted to fight for her, I knew that thug she loved so much wouldn't give me an opportunity to be around her. I had fucked up on that front and had allowed my jealousy to linger undetected for too long. Now, I was walking into another battle that was set up for me to lose too. When I made it over all the broken glass and flipped coffee table to where his room was located, the door was ajar but there was no light coming from the room.

I was a little apprehensive to enter but against my better judgment, I proceeded into the dark room. Once I made it into the room good, I stumbled over something, nearly landing face down on the carpet. Once my hands were planted on the ground, I could feel wetness soaking up between my fingers. I instantly jumped up and went to the bedside table to turn on the lamp. The scene the light revealed made my stomach turn. Daylen laid behind the door with a stainless chef's knife plunged into his stomach. I instantly grabbed my phone out of my pocket. I had powered it off due to Daylen calling so many times. I waited the short time it took to power on the phone and instantly dialed 911. I hadn't realized I was crying until I heard the emergency dispatcher asking me to calm down. I was trying to do everything she asked me to do. Once she realized I wasn't going to be much help, she advised me that emergency vehicles were on the way and to not move Daylen at all. I looked at my lover as small shallow breaths escaped him. Out of all the days, he had to do something this dumb and now I was even more hurt. I hadn't given my own son the courtesy of calling 911, but here I was again for the second time in twelve hours, crying my eyes out for someone I claimed to love.

It felt like hours but it took a little under ten minutes for the paramedics to arrive. Watching them hook Daylen up to the gurney and slide the oxygen mask over his face, I felt numb. Here was another person in my life that I could possibly be losing. This made me feel like he had been calling me to stop himself, but how would I ever know if he didn't pull through this? I watched them wheel him out to the ambulance and load him in. One of the EMTs informed me that they were taking him to Halifax, and I told them I would meet them down there. They took off moments later in route to the hospital. I wasn't going though. I would let God do his thing, and if he spared Daylen's life, I would make a conscious effort to do right by him or at least try.

****

After three hours of cleaning up Daylen's mess and showing no signs of sleep, I sat on the couch, staring off into space. I had gone through Daylen's phone and despite the fact that we weren't a couple, it was kind of crazy to see all the text messages from different men soliciting for sex and time. And from his responses, he entertained these guys a little too much for my taste. Daylen better hoped he died or I was going to kill him myself. I decided to text Candice. I didn't know if she would respond. I mean it was five something in the morning, but I would be happy if she did. After sending the text, I tried with all my might to stay awake, but as the sun begin to peek through the blinds, I fell asleep. When I woke a few hours later, it didn't take my brain long to process what had transpired. I took my time showering and getting ready to check Daylen's status. A part of me wanted him to die because of the dumb shit I had found in his phone, but another part of me wanted him to make it, so I could show him the love I hadn't been. I finished showering and getting myself together to head back down to the same hospital that I had spent the previous day at. I grabbed my phone and Daylen's phone, which was near dying and headed out the door.

Fifteen minutes later, I pulled up to the emergency room entrance. I found a spot right off the entrance ramp and made my way inside to the check in window. After a short wait, the admittance nurse gave me the floor information on Daylen, and I made my way towards the elevators. It felt different today riding up. I didn't know if he was ok, but I hoped that today's visit wasn't another crushing blow to my heart. Despite how I felt about him talking to other guys or him sometimes acting like we were more than we were, I did care about Daylen. When the doors opened up, the walk to his room seemed daunting. I didn't know what I was walking into. When I finally made it to his room, he was resting so serenely. I think I preferred him like this to be honest. I just stared at him upon entry because I did not want to disturb his rest. There were no machines hooked up to him, but I could see an IV drip going and I assumed that was standard with knife victims. I wanted to sit and stay but with him resting, I didn't want to just sit here either. As I debated on heading for the door, it was like Daylen could feel I was in the room because his eyes fluttered opened and he was fixated on me, but he didn't say anything.

Chapter 3

|Dasiah|

I had gone too hard last night, but who was going to tell me how to cope with my son's death? I had carried that baby for almost eight and a half months. My mouth was so dry like I had cotton growing from my throat. I had been feeling quite lonely; even with Lil by my side, I still felt like I had nothing and no one. I had been longing to be held, but I knew Khalil was trying to respect my space. I wish he would just act, but I also knew that I was nowhere near ready to be in a man's fold, even if I had history with that said man. I stretched my arms up and out from under the blanket. I had allowed the shots of gin to mask my pain last night and now the headache I had was being followed up by a massive hangover. I jumped out of bed and headed straight for the bathroom as I tried to keep my stomach's contents down my throat long enough to make it to the bathroom.

As soon as I made it in the bathroom and stood over the toilet, my mouth opened like a faucet and my stomach contents erupted into the porcelain apparatus. I hadn't had much of an appetite lately and I was dry heaving with little to nothing coming out. I cursed myself for drinking how I had. I had tears running down my face as I struggled to find relief. I hadn't heard him come in but felt his hands as they made circular motions on my back as he rubbed it. I couldn't have asked for a better person to have with me during this time.

"You ok, get it out." Lil coaxed me as he continued to rub my back. I think the sound of his voice helped me push out whatever was sitting on my stomach. Once I got up and looked in the toilet, I noticed that it had only been yellow stomach acid mixed with the remaining gin I had downed before going to bed. Lil had excused himself out the bathroom and I was now looking at my bloodshot eyes . The only trace of tears I had just been forced to cry was the small white trails that stained my face. I was mad at myself for getting drunk like I had. After dry heaving and finally getting something to come up, I felt gross. I washed my face and brushed my teeth before tying my hair in a top bun and turning the shower water all the way to scolding. It was something about a piping hot shower that always relaxed me and made me feel clean. I stepped under the shower waters steaming stream and allowed the heat to relax the queasy feeling in my stomach and to help relieve tension off my neck and shoulders. I don't know what happened, but I had slid down into the tub and was now in full fledge tears. I cried for my son, for my relationship. I wished my mama was still here. She always thought Jordan was the man for me and here I was feeling broken by the very man she praised.

I was so choked up by everything. I hadn't had this moment yet, and I was low-key happy it was happening right now in the shower. I silently sobbed to myself as the water had almost completely drenched my hair. I could care less about my hair though. I was concerned with my heart and my mind. I was young to most but to be enduring all this in such a short time period was like having a ton of bricks dropped right on top of me. I rubbed my empty abdomen remembering what Jayceon had felt like being inside me. I hadn't fathomed him not being here with me. My heart ached for his innocent soul. My son hadn't done anything to deserve any of this and here I was enduring all the pain. I sat in the tub with my knees up to my chest with my arms wrapped around them. The shower stream that was falling above me had begun to turn lukewarm, and I knew eventually whether I wanted him to or not, Lil would be in here to check on me. I finally stood to my feet as I finally lathered my pouf and washed my body a couple times before rinsing the soap off my wrinkling flesh. By now, the water made me shiver, and I knew I had been in too long, given the water was damn near ice cold. I hurried and grabbed my cheetah print silk robe and made my way back to my room.

I closed my door behind me and went and laid down on the bed. I knew the next few days were going to be tough, and I didn't have the energy to deal with it all, but I had to be strong. I was trying to gain my bearings when there was a light knock on my door. When Daniya's face appeared, I smiled. If I had anything to be happy about, it was the renewed relationship with my baby sister. She walked in my room and came and sat on the bed.

"How you feeling sis?" Niya asked, getting comfortable.

"Honestly... I feel like shit." I admitted.

"Well... I mean you went hard last night. I never knew you even smoked." She said with a smirk.

"Girl don't let this good girl image fool you. I know how to turn up and have a good time." I said, sitting up and propping myself up on a few pillows.

"Well I think I like you better high." She replied with a laugh.

"Yeah all my friends did too. I use to be a lil party animal when I was your age, but ma wasn't a fan though." I said, remembering all the trouble I got into behind Khalil and the shit we use to do.

"Mama did stay on y'all asses." Niya replied, shaking her head.

"I'm really sorry about Jayceon sis. I'll kill that pussy nigga for you." She said with venom laced in her voice.

I knew Niya was serious and given she had since dived deep into the streets, the thought of her handling street shit kind of tickled me.

"Baby sis, I know Glee got you thinking you a damn hot girl, but I don't want you to get in trouble behind me." I said seriously.

I watched as her brows furrowed before she spoke.

"You don't tell me what to do." She said, rolling her eyes at me followed by a huff.

I let out a sigh myself before reaching in my nightstand and pulling out a pre-rolled el po that I had started keeping since Khalil had been in the apartment. I used the lighter on the nightstand to light the blunt as Niya and I did a wake and bake before I started mentally preparing for the days and weeks ahead.

|Khalil|

A nigga was restless. I had been in lame ass Daytona for nearly two months, being selfless, but while I was a way from Da Burg, I was still making money. I wasn't sleeping for several reasons, and I had no plans of doing so until Keno was dealt with. And while Jordan was a bitch made ass nigga, he too had to feel my wrath, especially about Daish. This morning's conversation with my boy Glee had been on my mind since this morning. I was able to admit my faults, and while I had culpability in Dasiah and I's relationship ending, I placed most of the blame on her mother. Despite her being dead and gone, she had ultimately been the reason I let Daish go. She had approached me after finding out Dasiah was nearly nine weeks pregnant and had asked me for money to abort the baby. Me being me and not giving no fucks that this was my girl's mama, I cussed Ms. Kandi out like a dog. Then two days later, Dasiah called me, crying in the phone about her mama taking her down to the abortion clinic. I saw red, and I played my usual loving boyfriend role until about a week before she was set to leave for Bethune Cookman. I let the days count down until she had about three days left and broke it off with her. I knew Dasiah wasn't the one who initiated the abortion, but the fact that she didn't stand up for our unborn child left me feeling like she didn't love and care for me as she said.

Sitting here now, I knew that I had overreacted, and now I had reawaken all those old feelings in the last few weeks. Not touching her was killing me. I could smell her scent. When we did chill, she'd nestle up next to me, but I knew that given the current situation, she probably wasn't trying to fuck with a nigga like that. Right now, I knew my role, and I played it to the best of my ability. I knew she needed someone in her corner, and I was built for this shit. I was out picking up the money I had Tez Western Union me, so I could get Daish's and my attire for the small ceremony she had planned for later in the week. It would only be us four and a few of her friends from school that knew about her pregnancy. After the ceremony, I'd be giving her the money to break her lease, and we'd finally be headed back to St. Pete. My trigger finger had been itching ever since I found out Keno's bitch ass was out. That situation had to be dealt with immediately.

As I weaved in and out of the traffic, I made my way to the small Western Union, hoping the two grand I had Tez send would cover everything we needed until I could get back home. I was grateful for people like Tez. Cortez had been my best friend since our days at Happy Workers

Preschool, and he always keep it a buck fifty with a nigga. He had been A1 since day one and I never ever had to question my nigga's loyalty. He had been there through all my bullshit and he remained ten toes down. I would give my life for that nigga and I knew he'd do the same. Here my nigga was sending me some of my cash, just so I could handle business up here. While Glee was younger than us, he too had been solid and had been in our clique before he was even old enough to be. I loved my niggas and all my niggas loved me. I would put my life on the line for them all. I made it to Western Union and instead of two bands, this nigga had actually sent four. I knew he was hard of hearing and was trying to make sure I was straight. I fucked with my dawg for thinking ahead for me sometimes. I paid whatever fees I had to pay to get my money and headed to the mall to grab a few items for Jayceon's homegoing.

****

The apartment was already quiet but with me just there alone, I could hear everything going on outside the confines of the living room. Daish and Niya had gone out to grab their outfits and Glee was out running a few errands himself. I was rolling up as usual and trying to keep my mind off the impending situation back home. I had Tez's head on a swivel and had a few other people with their eyes and ears on that nigga Keno. He might have known by now that I hadn't been in the city the last few weeks, but just like he had Intel, so did I. I didn't want anybody else to act because I wanted to be the one to personally end this nigga's life. I was in my usual spot on the couch with the TV on and the mute button in use. I liked to be able to hear myself think.

Dasiah and I weren't together or anything but I had opened up my house to her. She had always crashed with me when I had my apartment, but now a nigga had a place I could call home. It could definitely use a woman's touch. My place was beautiful but the inside was less than beautiful because I rarely occupied the three bedroom, two and a half bath home. I stayed on the block or on the road making moves. I knew Daish would come in and make my house a home and more than likely make a nigga stay in the house more. I hated to admit it, but Dasiah made me soft. I had been doing my thug thizzle for the past three and a half years granted, but I would drop every hoe I had for Daish, no questions asked. She had my heart, and to be honest, she been had that shit before we were ever exclusive.

The way I felt about this woman was unexplainable. I had seen my share of heartache courtesy of the streets, but she made me feel whole; she made my darkest days seem brighter than I could ever see them alone. I wanted to make things right with Daish, and I knew I had to initiate the conversation, given I was the one who ended things between us three years ago. I wasn't ready for it but I knew it was necessary if we both would be around each other once we got back home. Once we gave Jayceon a proper send off, I would take a chance and talk to my one true love, just to see where she and I could take this thing. I was high as fuck but after weeks of not properly sleeping and binge smoking, I was feeling my body shutting down on me. I stretched out on the couch and for the first time since being here, I fell asleep.

|Daniya|

♫ "Baby it's yours

All yours

If you want it tonight

I'll give you the red light special

All through the night

Baby it's yours

All yours

If you want it tonight

Just come through my door

Take off my clothes

And turn on the red light" ♫

"Girl what the hell you know about a damn red light special?" Daish asked as we waited at a stoplight.

"Enough." I retorted, rolling my eyes and looking out the window still singing along with T-Boz, Chili, and Left Eye.

Her laughter filled the car as she drove through the light and towards the shopping plaza.

"What you thinking about grabbing for the service?" I asked, trying to pick her brain. so I'd know what to look for.

"I was thinking a nice navy or cobalt." Dasiah said as she turned into the entrance to the shopping plaza.

There was a Ross, TJ Maxx, and a Citi Trends amongst the different stores, and I knew I was sure to come in contact with something that would speak to me and be within my sister's color scheme. We found a spot close to the front of the plaza and got out.

"Let's meet at Ross. I need to go into another store for something." Dasiah said almost immediately.

"I mean, I guess. I thought we came here to do this together." I said with annoyance laced in my voice.

Dasiah waved me off as she headed in the opposite direction of me. I decided to try Citi Trends first. They usually had nice things for semi formal occasions, so I hoped I lucked up on the first try.

I knew the store back home was never in order; there was usually shit all over the store that made it next to impossible to find anything. This store was no different. Things were in disarray and on top of not being greeted upon entry, I would have much rather spend my money elsewhere than in here. After a quick walk through, I exited the store and headed to the next store. TJ Maxx was a little more inviting and the sales lady spoke to me upon entering.

That made a difference to me, speaking would either get you a customer or lose you one in my book. I found my way towards the junior misses section and started rummaging through the section that was marked large. Sifting through the latest season's plethora of options, my eyes landed on a navy blue sheath dress with a silver chain sewn at the top with pearls. I snatched the dress off the rack and draped it over my forearm as I checked the size. It was in my size and definitely appropriate for my nephew's service. I browsed a bit more, finding two more options but my first option was the clear winner. While I knew Daish wanted to meet up in Ross, I knew that I had found my outfit in here. I put the other two dresses on the nearest rack I could find before walking up to the register to pay. After a short wait in line and the sales lady complimenting my natural hair, she rung me up. I paid and headed to Ross to see if Daish was having any luck. I thanked the sales associate and left out headed in the direction to Ross.

"I really like the color." Daish gushed as she held up a basic normal fitted dress in a cobalt blue shade.

"I like." I said, watching her hold it up against her chest.

"Me too but I don't want to miss out on something else that might be in here. Can you help me look?" Daish asked as she draped the garment over her arm and proceeded to look through the different styles.

"You still a medium?" I asked.

Daish cut her eyes at me before answering.

"Yeah heffa, what you thought?" She replied with a roll of her eyes.

I laughed as I walked over to another dress rack and looked in the medium size section. Given we were well into the fall season, a lot of the colors were earth toned or floral prints, but I found a dress almost the same color as mine, just more regal. It had long sleeves with a swoop neckline. I loved the way the dressed look and was satisfied with my efforts to help my sister find a dress. I walked through the store in search for Dasiah. I had damn near walked the entire store before finding her in the shoe section, trying to match something to the first dress she had settled on. I knew she had given up trying to find something, so my additional option could possibly persuade her.

"Look at what I found." I said, showcasing the dress. I was practically swinging it in her face.

"Ooo... that's cute as hell." She said, snatching the dress out of my hand.

She ran over to a nearby mirror and held the dress up against her slim thick frame. I watched as she admired herself for a minute before disappearing back down the shoe aisle. I knew my choice had won because she had since deserted her first choice on a bench designated for trying on shoes. She emerged from the aisle with a shoe box in hand and made her way straight to the register. After she paid, we went to the Chinese restaurant that was also in the plaza. We ordered food for us and the boys and waited the ten minutes it took for them to prepare it.

"Sooo sissy, what's going on with you and Glee?" Daish questioned.

I hadn't realized that I was smiling until Daish smirked at me and said something.

"Man shut up!" I said, slightly embarrassed that just the thought of Glee had me showing my feelings.

"I'm just saying baby sis... you seem like y'all done got real close since I last saw y'all." She said.

She was right though. Glee and I had gotten super close since we were here last. So much so, I was about to go against respecting her apartment and get me some dick later.

"I mean... yeah of course we close, we do business together." I said, attempting to sugarcoat what it really was.

"Girl bye! I can see yo hips and ass filling out. I know what's really going on." My sister said with a smirk.

I looked away again, trying hard not to disclose the smile that was fighting to betray me.

"Ion know what you mean." I replied with the most serious face I could muster.

I want to burst out in laughter because despite not being close for so long, Daish could see right through me. Now I understood what Alani used to mean by she wished she had a sister. While it had only been a few months, I had a newfound respect for my only sister. I wished I had repaired our relationship much sooner, but now was a fine time to pick up on a relationship that I hadn't thought would ever develop. I was glad to have my sister. I felt like even at twenty, she was better equipped with knowledge from our mother. I wouldn't get those valuable lessons she got at the end of her adolescence, but I could obtain the same info via her. I did have Glee on my mind and regardless of what I tried to get myself to believe about my attraction to him, I couldn't deny the fact that I wanted him in more ways than one. We had never really discussed being exclusive and I wondered if he was waiting for my sixteenth birthday to arrive, just so he could be dramatic and make a move; however, he hadn't given any indication he was ready for all that.

"You can be secretive about your feelings all you want, but you wearing them mu'fuckas bold and brazenly for everyone to see whether you know it or not." Daish said with conviction before handing me the keys and heading to the counter to grab our food.

I made it to the car and unlocked the doors. As I got comfortable inside, I could see Dasiah carrying two bags with two trays a piece in each. I was more than ready to eat. I had been starving since earlier. She walked over to my side of the car as I rolled down the passenger's side window. She passed the two bags to me through the window before walking around and getting in. She fastened her seat belt before pulling out the parking lot of the shopping center.

****

When we got back to the apartment, it was nearly seven and Glee hadn't gotten back yet. Lil and my sister cozied up on the couch and were watching a movie. I had initially texted Raphael on our way here when I got the news about my nephew and let him know that I'd be in town; he had advised me to just hit him up anytime. I knew Raph would probably want to get high and we definitely had to catch up. I hadn't seen my dawg since I went back home. I shot him a text and a few seconds later, he replied, telling me to come on up.

I was in the room that had been mine while I was here and it would have been Jayceon's, seeing it half finished made my heart hurt. With Glee still out running errands and my unwillingness to participate as a third wheel to my sister and Lil, going to see my homie was right up my alley. I grabbed my hoodie, phone, and a couple El Productos. I walked over to the dresser where I had left my weed and grabbed a few nuggets out the sandwich bag. A girl would not be caught slippin' without basic necessities. I also needed my arsenal of snacks because Raph was bound to have some wild ass weed too, so the inevitable was bound to happen when my munchies kicked in.

I made my way to the designated cabinet for snacks. Our mama kept a snack cabinet when we were growing up. Dasiah and I would raid that mu'fucka every chance we got. Eventually, the snacks in the cabinet would be gone and my mama would refuse to restock it. We ended up just keeping our own snacks in our rooms, but it was funny to see her adopt one of our mother's small little things. I smiled at the memory as I grabbed a bag of hot popcorn, a Reese's, a couple packs of Fruit Roll Ups, and a pack of Famous Amos cookies. I made one last stop at the fridge to grab me a Zephyrhills water out of it.

"Where you headed?" Dasiah asked with her head turnt my way.

"Upstairs to see Raph for a minute." I said, looking under the sink for an old grocery bag.

"Oh ok... tell him I said hey." She said.

When I had gathered all of my provisions, I headed out the door and up the flight of stairs. When I got to Raph's, I knocked briefly before being greeted by the only person I really connected with while here.

"Lil' mama! What's happenin'?" Raph said, bringing me in for a hug.

"Nothing much homie, just out here trying to make sense of everything." I answer too honestly.

"Shit it be like that. I'm really sorry to hear about your nephew. Shit crazy." He said, shaking his head.

"Appreciate that man and yeah it is. When I catch that booty bandit ass nigga, Ima make his ass pay for all the shit he done did." I said with venom laced words.

Raph shook his head in agreement as he produced an already rolled blunt. I had since gotten comfortable on the couch and was already tearing the cancer paper out of the cigar I was rolling. Raph turned on the TV and lit the blunt he had up. I focused on finishing mine before he was passing his to me.

"You looking real good lil' mama." Raph complimented.

"I know. I been making some moves, and I finally can take care of myself like I want." I said, finishing up my roll.

"Well you lookin' good ma." He said as he passed me the blunt.

"Thank you." I said, taking the biggest pull off the potent ass cigar.

I let out a few smoke induced coughs as I allowed the weed to relax me.

"So you coming to the service right?" I inquired as Raph browsed the TV guide channel.

"Of course I am, ain't no way I'd miss that." Raph said, taking the blunt from me.

"Good, I know Daisha appreciates you just like I do." I honestly said.

"Man that shit real deal pissed me off. To be the one that found her like that still fucks with me dawg." Raph dropped his head and shook it as he spoke.

"Man I can't even imagine what that must have been like for you, but I'm glad you got to her when you did." I replied honestly.

Had it not been for Raph, Lord knows where Dasiah would be; shit we probably would have had two funerals weeks ago. I was forever grateful for him.

"Anybody at school heard from that pussy?" I inquired as I sparked up my blunt.

"Hell nah but some people say that Daylen know where he is. That fruitball had the nerve to be talking about the shit at school, just adding fuel to the fire. He pathetic as hell for that shit too." Raph fumed.

I was glad that once we properly laid my nephew to rest that this would be the last time I would ever be in this city unless my money habits brought me back. I wanted to enjoy Raph's company, but I knew I had to get back to the apartment soon. It was like my sister was on the same brain wave as me because I got a text from her.

Sis: Get back here ASAP. Khalil texted Glee where you went

Me: WTF!

I hated to leave in haste, but I figured it wouldn't hurt much if I stopped by to chill. What I hadn't factored was Lil snitchin' on a bitch and that made me feel some type of way. Glee wasn't even my nigga and the fact that he may or may not be mad had me hot. I didn't want to cut my time short with Raph, and I didn't want him to feel weird about our friendship; but I also didn't want to make Glee feel like something other than a friendship was going on between Raph and I. Had I known Lil was going to text Glee what I had going on, I would have texted Daish where I was going. I tried to keep up with what Raph was talking about, but my brain was overwhelming me.

"Yo big homie, Dasiah's ass need me for something. You gone be at the service right?" I asked, getting up mid smoke.

"Damn... you just sparked yours up though, and yeah I'll be there." He said, trying to pass the blunt back my way.

"Nah keep it." I said before giving him a hug and heading out the door. I was hoping Glee hadn't made it back yet as I made my way to Dasiah's apartment. I was trying to gather myself because I was really close to giving Khalil a piece of my mind. As soon as I turned the knob and entered, I had three sets of eyes on me. Dasiah's look was a sympathetic one, Khalil's eyes said nothing, and Glee's eyes were looking through me. I headed straight down the hall to the room and closed the door. Moments later, an angry Glee walked in. I braced myself for what he was about to say.

"You like trying a nigga huh?" He said with so much anger.

I was stuck, frozen. I didn't know what to say. How was I trying a nigga I wasn't even with?

|Keno|

I had been kicking it with the lil bitch from Gyros. Stasi was what her friends called her, but she answered to whatever I called her lil hot pussy ass. She was eighteen with her first child, and she had her very own section eight issued apartment. It came with all the fixings, roaches included. I stayed over a few nights and each time, I regretted staying. I had to shake my clothes off or shake out my shoes just to make sure I didn't take any of her pets home with me. We had just finished fucking and I was waiting on the tacos she promised a nigga. I was laying in the bed, looking up at the dingy ceiling, just thinking. Them pussy ass niggas were still M.I.A., but I knew they wouldn't be able to hide much longer. I would just enjoy some decent pussy and some fire ass head for now. Stasi walked in butt ass naked as she walked her cute ass over to the bed with a plate of tacos.

"Damn babygirl, you know how to treat yo nigga huh?" I said, taking a bite out the first taco. I watched her walk out the room again and then moments later, she was back with a glass filled with blue Kool-aid.

"Mmm yes! A nigga could get use to your young ass." I said, causing her to smile at me. I heard her daughter crying from the living room. She sucked her teeth before turning around to tend to her baby. I watched her plump ass shake as she walked away. From what she had told me about her situation, her and her daughter's father were on again off again, and he wasn't really involved with her or the baby. From the way I observed her talking to the poor baby, her ass didn't need no damn baby. She would usually just let her cry or talk shit about having to take care of her. I kinda felt bad for the lil baby, but I knew how bitches were with they kids, and I had my own babymama to belittle and bash. I finished the food and placed the paper plate on the nightstand next to the bed. I grabbed the half of blunt out the ashtray and sparked it up.

"Why you always ruining my time?" I could hear Stasi out in the living room, questioning a baby about something she had no control over. I was relieved this was just a fuck thang because I could never wife a bitch like this. I had nearly smoked the rest of the blunt before Stasi walked back in with a cotton robe on.

"You coming back later?" She inquired as she poorly tried to tidy up her room.

"Damn... you kickin' a nigga out and shit?" I said with an attitude.

"Nah, I ain't kickin' you out, but me and my girls gotta go fill some orders." She said as she wiggled her thick ass into a pair of jeans.

Stasi had told me how her and her friends boosted from local malls and stores and made money off of it. While I understood their hustle, it was hoodrat certified if you asked me. I got up out the bed and adjusted my johnson as I put on my own clothes. I had a few corners to bend myself, so I finished getting dressed before hugging Stasi and leaving.

The sun was hot as fuck today and we were literally a week away from it being December. I wanted to run down on the buddy I had stalking Khalil nem trap. I hadn't heard from the crackhead that would sell his own mama out in a few days, and I was worried he had been found out. I headed towards the area that I knew him and his fellow fiends hung out. I Lil Face was one of the local neighborhood fiends, and if you ever ran down on him, he would have this long drawn out rap that he had pretty much memorized. It was entertaining to watch him recite it to anybody that would stop and listen. He got his name Lil Face from the way his face looked since he had not one tooth in his mouth. His face had sunk in years ago from over usage of his preferred drug of choice and had created a permanent face deformity for the man. Like I said, if crack or money was involved, he would sell his own mother out if that meant he could get high. I started riding slower as I neared the oak tree that all the bums and basers alike would congregate at. As I scanned the sea of worn faces and drug induced stupors, my eye fell upon another dope fiend named Rascal that I knew ran with Lil Face. He was arguing with another lost soul when I grabbed his attention with my horn. He immediately forgot about whatever he was arguing with the other man about as he headed in my direction with a pep in his step.

"Keno my man! Whatcha got for me today." He said, exposing a grill that had more spaces missing teeth than a little bit.

"Ain't got shit for you man, where Lil Face at?" I asked, skipping all the pleasantries.

"Man I ain't seen Lil Face in a few days man. We smoked a big ass rock a few days ago, and I ain't seen that mushed faced mu'fucka since." Rascal said, wiping snot from his nose with the back of his hand as he leaned into my car.

To say I was disgusted would have been an understatement. Before Rascal could fix his lips to ask me for a dime, I peeled off, damn near running the man over. I wasn't sure where Lil Face was but his ass had better show up because if Khalil hadn't had him killed, I was going to do it myself. I rode to the next spot, which was the bitch boys' lil trap, just to see if this fiend had switched his loyalty to the opposing team. Crack was a hell of a monkey to get off your back and I knew he would pledge his allegiance to whomever possessed the biggest pull for his addiction. As I rolled down the street I had put Lil Face on, the trap looked dead. There was no one in sight, up or down the street either.

I pulled over, killed the engine, and just sat and observed. I hoped I could catch Lil Face zombied out somewhere. Nothing was going on, not even a dice game. Being in jail so long, I wasn't use to the silence in the hood. Even though this technically wasn't my hood, I had never known it to be this quiet during the day. I was parked a little up the road but still had a plain view of the trap that Khalil ran and there was no activity going on. I didn't even see a single car in the dirt lot next to it. Shit was definitely weird.

I felt my phone buzzing in my pocket and pulled it out. It was a text from Stasi's fine ass. I was still getting use to this camera phone shit, so the picture of her in the blue lace lingerie had me adjusting myself. Baby girl looked good. I shot her one of the preloaded emoticons and clicked the phone off. I put my focus back on the trap as I notice someone walking up towards it. The person knocked a couple times, stood, and waited. After another set of knocks with no answer, they turned and walked away. Something wasn't right, I thought after sitting there for about twenty more minutes before driving off. There was no way Khalil had left his trap this vulnerable. I hoped Lil Face hadn't fucked up.

Chapter 4

|Daylen|

I was getting real sick and tired of these damn doctors and nurses. I couldn't wait till I could go home. I did like that I was being waited on hand and foot though. Even Jordan had been here since I opened my eyes. I don't know why I stabbed myself, but the minute I thrusted the blade in my gut, I instantly regretted it. I was so glad Jordan came in when he did. Lord knows what may have happened. Jordan was sitting in the chair nearest the window and his nose was practically in his phone. I could have sworn I saw him smiling at it a few times, but it could have easily been all the damn Tramadol I was being administered. I shook it off as me being loopy, but I could see something alive in his eyes again. I would most definitely be putting on my inspector gadget hat when I was up to it to find out what this nigga was up to.

"Babbbe." I cooed.

I saw Jordan cut his eyes at me before responding.

"Man wassup?" He asked dryly.

I didn't like his response, so I turned my head and proceeded to pout. He finally sucked his teeth and started giving me the attention I liked.

"Man stop that shit bae. What you need?" Jordan coaxed as he came over, lifting my hand and kissing it. My attitude quickly dropped and I smiled at him.

"I really want some Chinese food. I'm tired of this hospital food." I said honestly.

"Well Chinese it is. I'll run by the house too to grab you a few things." He said with a smile. He seemed happy to help, but I also knew Jordan. He would say and do whatever to get what he wanted, but I brushed it off, so I could get what I wanted.

I gave him a sweet smile before getting comfortable again under the cover. He placed a kiss on my forehead and then headed out. Jordan wasn't slick by a long shot. I knew something or someone had his attention, and I was damn sure about to find out. I'd be damn if I let this Docker pants wearing, shirt tucking undercover mu'fucka play me again. I layed back and focused in on the daytime soaps and drifted off to sleep.

****

"We've been monitoring his signs and the text results were positive Doctor."

"You sure he tested positive for it?"

I could hear the nurse and the doctor discussing my hidden medical prognosis, but I continued to pretend like I was sleep. I didn't want to have this conversation for the umpteenth time. I didn't want treatment and that was that. I knew what my fate was, hence why I took pride in stirring up trouble at every corner. It would be a matter of time before I succumbed to the autoimmune disease. I kept my eyes closed as they finished their conversation. I knew I wouldn't be able to dodge it much longer, but I'd try my damndest to prolong it as long as I could. To add to their conversation, I braced myself before pushing the loudest fart I could muster out of my ass. I wanted these mu'fuckas outta here.

"Ooh... someone's gassy!" I heard the nurse say before spraying a bit of the room spray I had Jordan bring down, so it would at least smell like home while I was here. I finally heard them clear out as a smile came across my face, and I drifted back to sleep.

|Alani|

"Don't Stop! Don't Stop! Ooohhh you better not stop!" I growled in Mack's ear.

He was digging in me like a half gallon of butter pecan ice cream. He made every stroke count. I finally got on top and took control. I rode this nigga like a buckin' bronco. Mack grabbed a fist full of my sandy red hair and yanked my head back as I rode him for dear life. I hadn't realized how much I missed his dick until I was riding it again. I licked my lips before bending down and sucking on his neck, making my way down his chest. He picked up the pace even though I was on top. I hated losing control. Mack started throwing his hips up, making me bounce on him. I could feel my nut coming as he continued to thrust his eight and a half inch johnson inside me. This dude knew how to fuck and I loved a good partner. I hopped off from riding and took his rock hard tool in my mouth. I was about to eat this dick like a popsicle on a hot summer day. I had just started going in when Mack's phone started going off. At first, he ignored it but by the third ring, he picked up. I kept sucking, hoping my skills would make him hang up the phone. Yet when he practically yanked his meat out of my mouth, I was so mad; all I wanted to do was make him come. It started to look like my plans weren't going as I wanted them to. I went to speak but he put up his index finger, signaling me one minute.

I immediately turned into the 16 year old girl that I was, pouting, huffing, and rolling my eyes. I looked at Mack hoping my tactics were working, but he was just shaking his head at me as he began dressing while still listening to his caller. I couldn't believe he was really about to go. I had already missed out the first time this opportunity came and now he was skipping out on me. I sat in my bed damn near naked as I watched him peel a couple hundred dollar bills off the bankroll he had and placed the money on my nightstand. I was pissed because this was not how my day was suppose to go. He chucked the deuces at me as he walked out the side door of my house and out to our backyard where he had parked his car.

I yelled out in frustration as I grabbed my towel and a bra and panty set and headed to take a shower. After washing my body twice and rinsing off, I put on my bra and panties and grabbed my pink cotton robe off the back of the door. My house was vacant; everybody was out doing their own thing. While I wanted to enjoy the house a while longer, them hot two hundred dollars were burning a hole on top of my nightstand and I knew a lil shopping would make me a lil happier. I finished dressing as I slid my feet in my black

Donna Karan kitten heels that matched my black halter jumpsuit and paired it with the tennis bracelet and diamond stud set that my dad had gotten me for my birthday. I looked at myself in the mirror one last time before walking out the door headed to It's Fashion boutique in search of some much needed retail therapy.

****

Mack's measly two hundred was spent ten minutes in the store. I had a lil change saved, so I was able to cover the rest of my items. I opted to stop at the local Italian place Giuseppe's that was located in the same plaza as the clothing store. I really loved their calzones and needed one before I went home. I went inside and placed my order and decided to wait outside. Most of the time, this place took forever to make an order of breadsticks, so I knew I could step outside and hit the blunt I had tucked securely in my purse. I had been outside the restaurant maybe five minutes before hearing and seeing a familiar group of lil boys. My big headed brother was the ringleader of this dysfunctional band of friends. Just like my brother and I, his friends, Niko and Miles, came from similar situations, except their moms were legit working as nurses and other legitimate hustles that kept them away from home. Our mom was a straight hoe in an abusive relationship that couldn't control either of her kids. I kept hitting my blunt as my brother Alvin walked up to me.

"Wassup sis? That shit smell good." He said, referencing my latest cuff out of Mike's stash.

"Hey y'all." I said, addressing all three of them.

Niko, who was the shortest out the group, smiled a flawless smile, exposing his Colgate white smile. He was mixed with hair like a cherub. Miles and my brother were about the same height but they differed in so many other ways. Miles had a gap but his smile was still impeccable. He had a cocoa complexion and hands that could easily palm a basketball. He's also the oldest out of the group, yet his ass ran behind my twelve year old brother. Miles stared at me like he'd already fucked me a thousand times in his head, and I couldn't blame him for wanting to. Had the world not seen what I had been blessed with? My baby brother was the color of brown sugar when it got wet and his almond shaped eyes had everyone wondering if he was half Asian. However, my brother took after his dad's side of the family, and they were straight niggas. My brother's grill was all fucked up after countless bike accidents and running from the police in stolen cars. He had more chips than a poker game.

"What the hell y'all up to?" I inquired, passing the blunt to my brother.

"Shit looking for a car to snatch sis. You heard Lil had Tez relocate?" Alvin said, hitting the blunt.

"What... why?!" I asked as my brain went back to the plan Keno had in motion. I knew he had Lil Face placed there, and if they had relocated, it meant Lil Face was dead or he had switched sides.

"Sis all I know is we went to cop some weed from Tez by Rajax and he told us he had to move the trap. Didn't he?" My brother said before waiting for his friends to nod and agree.

"Damn... well, I'll have to find out where it's at." I said, trying to not sound irritated with this news.

"Well it can't be far from the last one sis. Tez was literally waiting at the store within five minutes of us calling."

I finished smoking with my brother and his friends before grabbing my food and walking back home. I would have to spend all day tomorrow digging up as much information on where this new trap was, and I was definitely curious if my cousin knew that they had relocated. I would text him later and let him know what was what.

|Glee|

Nelly's Country *Grammar* was blazing through the speakers of my car as I bent a few corners. While I wasn't home where everything was familiar, I had a natural sense of direction. I could get around anywhere and if I had to ask for directions, I was honestly lost. I had gone to the Volusia mall and grabbed a nice Ralph Lauren button up with a pair of matching Polo slacks out of Dillard's. I also made detours to a few stores that I knew Niya loved, and given her birthday was a week away, I wanted to grab her a few gifts. I had been focused on picking the charms for her bracelet I was getting her in Kay's when Lil's text hit my phone, telling me Niya was blatantly trying me. I had all nerve to take all the shit back that I had already bought, but I wasn't that type of nigga. I finished picking her charms and let the sales lady wrap it up for me. If Niya really thought she was going to try me like she was, she had a nigga all the way fucked up. Yeah I liked her ass, but lil mama wasn't about to play me. I knew the nigga Raph had looked out for her while she was up here and shit, but he was still a nigga. Regardless if he ain't ever try her, it could be a matter of time before he did.

I paid for the charm bracelet and headed straight to my whip. I hoped Niya had sense enough to beat me back to the apartment, but in case she needed a reminder of what the fuck we had going on, I had no problem refreshing her memory. I had never really let anyone in my life as much as I had allowed Niya to be, so getting informed that my future bitch was underneath the next nigga had me hot. Don't get me wrong, I trusted her, but I didn't trust other niggas besides the niggas I ran with. The nigga could have the best intentions, but I didn't give a fuck. I floored it back to the apartment, hoping she would be waiting for me at Dasiah's. When I pulled up, I took the time to secure her gifts in my secret compartment in my trunk. It usually housed drug packs but until December fourth, it would house Niya's gifts. I got out with my Dillard's bag and made my way up to the second floor apartment. When I knocked, I was met with an eye roll from Dasiah. I knew she probably had an attitude because my boy had let me know what her sister was doing, but I didn't give a fuck. If Niya was going to be my lady, she was going to have to behave like she had a man even if she didn't.

"Girl fix yo face." Lil commented while shaking his head as he watched Dasiah throw her attitude around. She cut her eyes at him before plopping back down on the couch and putting her attention back on the TV.

It was just them in the living room like when I left, so I went back to the room to put my bags in there and to see if Niya was in there. When I pushed the door open and the room was empty, my attitude grew bigger. I grabbed some bud and a gar and went and joined Khalil and Dasiah in the living room. Daniya had a nigga all the way fucked up. I would just wait until she walked her pretty ass back in this apartment then she was going to be in for a rude awakening. She had only seen the nice side of a nigga; but today, I was going to straighten her, so she never tried me like this again. Another thirty minutes passed before Niya made an appearance back at the apartment and she was clearly high as fuck. She walked in and all three of us turned and looked at her. I knew she was trying to read our expressions, but I was looking through her ass at this very moment. I didn't know if she was ready for what I was on. I watched as she took off down the hall. As I heard the room door close, I hopped to my feet and headed to the room to address some shit.

"You like trying a nigga huh?" I said with so much anger.

She was stuck, frozen. She couldn't bring herself to say anything.

"Since you can't talk, allow me to elaborate lil mama." I calmly stated.

"You act like you my nigga." Niya said with an attitude.

"Ohh, so you think we just fuckin' on each other? Nah... you got me fucked up. Ion fuck on people. No I ain't yo nigga yet, but I expect you to behave like you do got a man." I said seriously.

"Well Glee... damn... this is all new to me. Plus I ain't do nothing wrong." She tried reasoning with me.

"I don't doubt you did anything wrong, but how you know that nigga Raph won't try you huh?" Before she could reply, I continued. "Furthermore, I stick my dick in you. I don't even want you around another nigga that would think he remotely have a chance of finessin' you out that pussy. I'll kill a nigga bout you Niya." I said seriously. Her eyes widen at my last statement, but I meant every fuckin' word. I had put my name on that pussy. I knew her ass would never willingly submit to the next nigga, but niggas would take some shit from a bitch if they felt like it was owed.

"Glee I get what you saying, but you ain't giving me no credit. I ain't stupid... damn." She said, rolling her eyes at me.

I found that shit cute when she started throwing her attitude around, but her ass wasn't gone shake shit over here.

"You mine and Ion want you hanging with no niggas other than my niggas."

"Well what if I don't want to be yours?" She asked, challenging me. If Niya thought she wasn't mine, she had another thing coming; but I wanted to see where her mind was at, so I played along.

"Then I guess you don't want to be mine. I'll just go holla at Alani when we get back to Da Burg." I said with a straight face. I watched as her face scrunched up and turned sour quick.

"You got me all the way fucked up Shamar if you think you gone just go fuck with that hoe after you been dickin' me down." I was amazed at the sudden fire in her, but I knew she was mad because she had used a nigga's government name. I tried to keep a poker face but I ended up cracking a smile, which resulted in her punching me hard as fuck in my arm.

"Man I swear yo ass need to let me take bets on yo ass and put you to work." I joked as I went over and pulled her off the bed and into my arms. She tried pulling away, but I tightened my grip on her.

"You like making me mad man damn." She whined.

"It's not even that man. I be trying to move a certain way, and it be unexpected shit that make a nigga have to reveal shit I wasn't ready to say or do. But I really don't like niggas having access to you regardless of what he done did for you in the past... a nigga's intentions could change. I know you wasn't dressing like this when yo ass was up here. Nigga definitely lookin' at yo ass now." I said matter factly.

She sucked her teeth and said, "Raph ain't never tried me and he damn near twenty five years old. He just cool. If we were official, I would never be out disrespecting you in anyway." She looked me dead in my eyes when she spoke and for some reason, I believed her. I felt in my heart that she was supposed to be mine. I had planned on asking her when I surprised her on her birthday but any time was a good time. I skipped how I had planned on asking her and blurted out...

"Niya, you gone be my lady or what?" She started acting like she was thinking about it before a big ass cheesy grin appeared on her face.

"Man stop playing with me, you already know I wanna be." She said, wrapping her arms around my neck and kissing my lips.

She did a quick peck, but I decided to probe her mouth with my tongue as our tongues danced with one another. She sucked on my lips and that shit was deadass turning a nigga on; but I refused to disrespect Dasiah by fucking her little sister in the room intended for her son. I broke the kiss and looked Daniya dead in her eyes, admiring her beauty. I was going to do anything and everything that was required to make her happy. She was going to be my lil Bonnie. I smiled at her, admiring my new wifey as her eyes showed me our future. I walked her over to the bed and positioned her in front of me, so I could cuddle her from the back. She nestled into my body as we connected like puzzle pieces. She was right here in my arms where she was supposed to be and that's where she was gone remain.

|Jordan|

I went to grab Daylen some food, and in the midst of trying to show him I was trying to support him, I was enjoying the conversation Candice and I was having. She had been the one getting me through having to involuntary go down and check on Daylen. I would usually go to the Chinese restaurant by campus, but after Candice said she would be going on break soon, I thought to order Daylen's food from the restaurant directly across the street from the McDonald's. While China One was the better tasting of the two, China Star would have to do because I was going to get as much time with Candice as I could. I didn't feel bad for using Daylen. This latest stunt from him had shown me that he wasn't stable enough to handle anything that could potentially develop if I eventually felt the need to be my authentic self. For now, I would occupy my time trying to get to know Candice more and seeing where things went with us. As I pulled into the parking lot of the Chinese restaurant, I sent Candice a text, letting her know I wasn't far as I exited my vehicle to place my take out order.

Once my order of fried chicken wings and shrimp fried rice was placed, the Asian man told me that it would be ten minutes, and I walked the short distance to the popular burger chain. It wasn't busy as I waited for a car to back out of a space. I spotted Candice sitting outside at a table eating. She spotted me and waved as a smile came across her face. She was beautiful. Her peanut butter complexion and her big doe eyes drew me in. I returned a warm smile her way as I came closer to where she was sitting. She stood and gave me a welcoming hug as I squeezed her as we separated. I sat down across from where she was enjoying a medium fry and a chocolate fudge sundae. She was working on a crossword puzzle but promptly closed the book and focused on me.

"So you really came to see little oh me?" She said in her sweet voice. I watched her dip a fry in her sundae as she stared me dead in my eyes.

"Man I had to. You been keeping me interested since we started texting." I said honestly.

She looked away shyly as she used her hand to move the hair that had fallen in her face out of her way.

"Well you are definitely interesting too. I remember when I got into robotics and I thought I would be the next Bill Nye." She said, referencing to a conversation we had a few hours prior. That single conversation had me wide open. I had only met girls that were a little into what I was into, but

Candice shared a true interest in a lot of the same things I did.

"Bill's cool. I studied a lot of Subrahmanyan Chandrasekhar's work growing up." I replied, thinking of the hours of research I did on the astrophysicist as a kid.

"I've never met anyone into science as much as me. I'm a natural born nerd." She said, revealing her flawless smile.

"You definitely don't fit the bill to be a nerd... you're gorgeous." I schmoozed.

I watched as she checked the time on her phone. We spent the remainder of her break discussing different experiments we had conducted throughout school. By the time the seven minutes were up and we had gone our separate ways, I could still feel her body pressed against mine from the hug we shared before she left. I could get use to having a woman's warm embrace around again, but I didn't want or need Daylen's interference. It was time to cut ties with Daylen and try my luck in love with a woman more compatible with where I saw myself. I grabbed Daylen's food before hopping in my car and heading back to the hospital.

Chapter 5

|Dasiah|

Lil had me all the way fucked up by ratting my sister out to Glee. While I knew how this shit worked and had once been unofficial with Lil when I first started seeing him, he had explained to my young ass exactly what it was. I knew Glee from being the lil bad ass kid that would do anything to be down with Lil and Tez, but his ass was young too. I was more than sure that he hadn't sat down with Niya and explained what was what. Had he, I knew my sister would have just left without announcing where she was going, just to avoid Lil being in her business. I now felt bad for asking where she was going. I was off my A game and I would have usually sent her a text. My present state of mind had me acting before thinking, and now I was mad at the one person who had been there for me during this difficult time. Lil was letting me have my moment because he could care less about how I felt about him telling Glee. In his mind, that was his little brother and no one was going to have him looking stupid.

I had retreated to the bathroom and was going to hang out in here until I felt like coming out. I wasn't looking forward to saying goodbye to my son; tomorrow was going to be tough. I lit my lemon citron candle, pulled out my hair straightener, and a blunt. My silky black hair was a weird consistency of curls. I had inherited the curls from my mom and the closest I could get to my Asian roots was if I straightened my hair bone straight, but once humidity touched it, it was a wrap. I sparked up the blunt and moved my ashtray closer to where I was preparing to do my hair. I was going to straighten my hair then wrap it so all I had to do was comb it out in the morning. I was going to try and sleep tonight, but I knew like that last few that sleep might not come.

The entire week I had been mentally preparing for the small intimate service I had put together. I had only extended invites to a few of my classmates who knew what had been going on with me. I still hadn't reached out to Jordan's mom, but I knew had he been honest with her, she would have called me by now. I didn't want to be the reason her views of her own son changed, but what Jordan had done to me would eventually be on front street for all to see. I was going to mourn my son properly then I was going to make sure Jordan got exactly what he deserved. I spent forty five minutes getting my hair to be how I wanted it. When I finally put up all the products and hair tools I used and had securely wrapped and tied my hair up, I resparked the blunt I had started off with but had neglected while I did my hair and prepared for whatever Khalil would be on when I exited the bathroom. I didn't want to argue at all and quite frankly, since Niya and Glee hadn't gotten into a shouting match with one another, I assumed it was safe to come out. Hell if they weren't mad and arguing about it, then I sure as hell wasn't worrying about it.

When I walked out the bathroom, there was laughter and joking coming from the living room. I stood at the edge of the hall entryway as I observed my sister and Glee practically devouring each other's face. It was as if Khalil could feel my presence in the room because he looked right over at me and just stared at me. My instincts were prompting me to shoot a bird at him, but I didn't. I just smirked at him, causing him to do the same. Khalil and I could never stay mad at one another. The only time Khalil had stayed mad was when I got the abortion. That incident ended us. While I had wanted to work it out and had even told him we could have another baby, Lil wasn't trying to hear none of that. Till this day, I wished I would have stood up to my mom. I would probably be a mother of a couple of Khalil's kids. While he had been someone my mother viewed as negative, he had been the most positive thing to enter my life. I finally walked over to where he was sitting and he willingly moved over, so I could sit next to him.

"You done being mad big head?" He playfully said.

I cut my eyes at him before smirking at him.

"I'm straight."

He naturally rested his hand on my thigh as he passed me a halfway smoked blunt.

I gladly obliged as I allowed the potent weed relax my mind. I looked over as Glee and Niya were all over each other, laughing amongst themselves. While my ass was in the bathroom mad at Lil, these two had kissed and made up. Even though Glee was his own man, it was hard to forget that Khalil was like a mentor to Glee, so he would protect Glee against anyone even my sister. I would definitely be bringing it up at a later date. We all chilled for a bit before we all retired to our designated sleeping areas. As I layed in bed thinking about tomorrow, I said a prayer for strength as I drifted off to sleep.

|Keno|

Lil Face had to be dead. There was no way I had spent all day and most of the night looking for this nigga. It was damn near one thirty in the morning and no one that knew the vivacious buddy had seen him since a few days ago. Shit was starting to look weird. I had even rode back through the block where those pussies were known for being and the trap they used was dark as fuck. I was convinced now that the baser I had chosen had been compromised.

"Fuccck!" I cussed out loud as my fist slammed down on the steering wheel. Even when I thought I was up in points on this nigga, he managed to be steps ahead. I hated this nigga for his hustler's ambition and his all around demeanor. Even as kids, this nigga thought he was better than everyone. He may have had the personality, but the nigga was low-key hating on me. I didn't care what nobody said. While I had only been slangin' small shit starting out, Khalil and Tez rose up in the streets in a short amount of time, doing the same shit I was doing. They had even plugged in that lil jit Glee when he was fifteen. All those times I had gone over my people's house, I had peeped what was going on and wanted a piece of the pie, but them pussy ass niggas were hating hard. The day I tried to rob them was only after those pussies had jumped me after they caught me catching a few of their regulars. I knew the shit was going to get under their skin seeing me do it, but I didn't give a fuck, The way I saw it, we all could eat. After making sure that fuck nigga Khalil saw me blatantly disrespecting his block, I guess the nigga couldn't handle it, so he tried to shoot me.

At the time, my son King was one and his mom Eve and I had never been on good terms. After about five months of digging in her, Eve ended up pregnant and at the baby shower, I found out her and Khalil were first cousins. The shit was crazy and just added to both of our hatred for one another. Honestly, had I known she was his cousin, I would have done that hoe dirtier than I had and she damn sho' wouldn't have had my seed. When the shooting happened, he had been wildly shooting at me and I was trying to land a shot to his head; but instead of hitting him, my bullet hit his lil chinky bitch's friend and the bitch died. I took off from the scene, but later found out I had shot her in the heart. I didn't feel bad though. She should of had her fast ass in the house or something.

A month later, I was booked for a robbery that they couldn't prove I did, but because I had a record and fit the description, they threw my ass in jail. I never put up a fight and I just did the time. I had done the crime but I denied, denied, and denied and caught a break when I ended up with four years. After doing my time, I stepped back in these St. Pete's streets, ready to finally knock Khalil off his high horse. As I cruised back towards my mom's, I received a text from Alani with a 911 page, and I promptly called her.

"What it is cuz?"

|Alani|

I spent all day trying to locate where the new trap was. After a few questions to one of my home girls, she told me the new spot was off Highlands and that it was a whole process to get served. She said Tez was being cautious because they had to get rid of one of the buddies after they violated their last spot by spying on them. I already knew it was Lil Face; that alone didn't completely confirm that he was dead but knowing Lil, he had that nigga murked. The news here didn't report every time they found a dead body on the Southside, so it was possible his body had been discovered and that the community would never know. I was in the process of rolling up when I shot Keno a text, letting him know it was important, I added 911, so he knew it was serious. Within seconds, his name appeared on my screen. I picked up and put the phone on speaker.

"What it is cuz?"

"Shit cuz but we got a problem."

I heard Keno let out a sigh before he instructed me to continue.

"Well Alvin nem told me that Tez was told to move the spot. My home girl said that they found out one of the buddies was spying, so I think Lil Face ass is dead cuz." I said, sealing and then sparking my blunt as I got comfortable in my bed.

"Fuck man! That baser had one job, and I bet his dumb ass got high and started running his mouth. I know they think a mu'fucka was trying to get the ups on they operations, but my revenge coming at ol' girl party." My cousin stated matter factly. I just got higher while I listened to him rant.

I knew one thing he said was true, revenge would be at Niya's party front and center. She could have just told a bitch she was feeling Glee, and I probably would have suggested we fuck him together; but knowing Niya's prude virgin ass that would have never happened. I chopped it up with Keno a few more minutes as he vented his frustrations about Lil Face. While my cousin was handsome, he was dumb. Any nigga that had ever come at Khalil and his crew had fallen. There had been plenty shootouts on the block behind niggas coming at Khalil. Keno should have known Lil Face was going to inadvertently tell on his own self. I wanted my cousin to get his get back, but I damn sure wasn't going to be caught in him and Khalil's bullshit. I had bigger fish to fry with my ex-best friend. I finished talking to Keno; he told me to keep my ears open for anything else regarding the trap. I promised him he'd be the first person I hit up if something else happened. We ended our call and I put out the remainder of the blunt I had.

All my regular niggas that I kept in rotation were all unavailable. All I had was time to think about the upcoming week. We had literally planned this ambush a month ago. While my intentions were to just beat Daniya's ass for how she handled me in front of Glee, I knew my cousin wasn't coming to just fight. Keno got off on inciting chaos, and after talking to Keno, I knew the next time him and I linked up, it would be to carry out our plans. I looked over at the Lisa Frank calendar I had hanging up on my wall, and the date December 4th was circled with a red crayon. The fourth was Daniya's birthday, and I would bet my last dollar this would be a birthday she never forgot.

|Daylen|

I was released late last night due to crowding issues. I guess Halifax was done helping my black ass because I was on my couch stretched out, fighting to get comfortable. I would have much rather be in my bed but due to my injuries, I was unable to get in my bed, given it was so high off the ground. I would have most likely fell out of it and would have probably busted my stitches open. I could see that Jordan was trying, but I could also see a new light glowing in his eyes. Trust and believe, it had nothing to do with the fact that he was helping me. I swore when I got better, I was gonna investigate everything. I wanted him to remember who had always been there for him. Even with Dasiah out the picture, my mind had been wondering had it really been about her. Maybe I too was a pawn in Jordan's sick twisted game. Hell he was definitely one in mine, and I would most definitely be the one getting the last laugh. Jordan had stepped out to visit campus he claimed, but I couldn't be a hundred percent certain. I made a mental note to try and catch him in his lies later today.

Before I left the hospital, the doctor treating me suggested I speak with a counselor in regards to my medical condition that I had kept disclosed up until now, but they had found out due to my blood work. The counselor that they appointed to speak with me had come at me all wrong, and I asked his pelican faced ass to leave my room. I didn't feel the need to disclose my medical status to anyone. Half the niggas I fucked with deserved everything they got. They didn't care about me; hell the person who had given me the incurable disease hadn't told me. I just got really sick one day and had to be rushed to the hospital. When I found out what was really wrong with me, I lost it. I was only a kid, but my secret lover Alton had neglected to tell me that he was a walking incurable disease host. I was from Atlanta and had decided against my mother's wishes to remain there for college. When I met Alton my last semester of my senior year, he had come to me with more than the love and affection he claimed to have for me; unbeknownst to me, Alton jump started my life in a crazy downward spiral.

I had always felt different from my brothers. I wasn't a sports fanatic, wasn't checking for females, and enjoyed activities that my brothers wouldn't dare do. My oldest brother Daniel had been killed in a car accident my sophomore year in high school, and while I had never vocally said I was gay, my big brother just knew. He hadn't been judgmental or treated me any different. He just told me to be careful. From then on, I was more confident in who I was. Even at eighteen, I felt like I was a good judge of character; but four months into dealing with Alton and discovering not only did he have a whole wife and three kids, the nigga was also HIV positive. The day I collapsed and had to be rushed to the ER had been the scariest day of my life and it ultimately changed my life too. That day I had to watch my mama cry so much that she had enough tears to fill a lake. I had never seen my mother cry like she had, but she told me we would get through this and up until now I had been. Even though my drug abuse and alcohol consumptions added to my high levels of stress, the fact that I wanted genuine love and had yet to receive it was the reason I was healing from a self inflicted knife wound. The reason I hid my status was because down low men treated me like their dirty little secret and I liked having my own dirty secret.

I never got why down low men wouldn't just live in their truths, but for some reason, I was attracted to them. I think it was the fact that I knew their secret. And while Alton had broken me down to my core, he had also gave me life to be a menace in the lives of other down low men trying to have their cake and eat it too. I never disclosed my condition because these nasty ass niggas never asked. While they were courting women and making kids, they were walking around with something worse than the common cold. Even though I knew how it felt for someone to not disclose their status, it had only made me follow queue and do the same. If Alton didn't feel the need to tell me, why would I tell these niggas I was dealing with? Half of them dogged women, so whenever they found out they had it, I'm sure they would blame their latest flavor of the week. They never thought of me. I was the "homeboy" they all liked to fuck in private but dap up in public. I was never a flashy gay. I still dressed in baggy jeans and wore the current male fashion, but I would spice it up with one female accessory from time to time.

It would be a matter of time before Jordan found out it didn't pay to be nasty. The entire duration of whatever this was we were doing was all a lie. Just like every man before him, he had used my mind and body for his own personal reasons. While I filled voids and took dick in nearly every hole in my body, I had yet to find a dick big enough to fill the hole I had in my soul. No man had ever loved me unconditionally. I felt like every time I found someone who showed potential, they would say all the right things to lure me in and eventually they'd play me, not knowing that I was holding the winning cards and had control over their lives. Given I've always maintained my health, I never appear sick. Anytime I dealt with someone new, usually our first encounters are strictly something that keeps them in the clear from contracting it from me. But once I started to peep how these assholes were handling me, I decided to get infinite revenge on men that decided they would use me up and then get rid of me.

No one had yet to put it together, but I knew two men that I had dealt with, one here in Daytona and one back home, that both had it. It was told to me that they both got it from women they had dealt with, so I knew that I could hide behind the fact that gay men weren't the only ones out here fucking off the chain, passing shit around. These women would be out here fucking every Tom, Dick or Harry and taking that shit back to they niggas and vice versa, except the boy pussy fucked the game up when we started getting the tough and rugged dope boy that loved sagging his pants and loved ramming his dick in male anal cavities too. I was so deep in my thoughts that I hadn't heard Jordan walking in, struggling to hold the bags from Winn Dixie.

I attempted to get up to help, but he told me to stay where I was and that he had it. With his back turned to me as he started putting away the groceries, a smirk crept across my face. I enjoyed the game I was playing and would soon be able to see the end results.

Chapter 6

|Daniya|

The small room at the funeral home that Dasiah had chosen for Jayceon's service suited the fifteen people that were in attendance. Most of the people there attended school with her and had been really upset about the situation. Glee and I sat in the first row right next to Dasiah and Khalil. We were waiting a few more minutes just in case anyone else was coming. Jordan wasn't anywhere in the building, and I better not had seen his ass in here. If he was dumb enough to show up here, he would be in for the ass whoopin' of the century. Looking around the service, I saw two familiar faces. Shayla was sitting over on the right side of the small room with a somber look on her face. And I spotted Raph a few pews back on our side. I hadn't seen him arrive, but I wanted to speak and thank him for coming to support us. I knew Glee did not want me to associate with him, but I was going to see Raph and say goodbye before going home. Despite how Glee felt and regardless of us being official, I hadn't been raised to turn my back on people who had proven they had my back. I planned on talking to Raph once the service was over.

Dasiah had gotten a flower arrangement in the shape of an angel with feathered baby blue wings. The body of the angel was made up of blue chrysanthemum flowers and a blue rose arrangement in the bottom corner to make it special. There were also an assortment of blue and white colored stuff animals aligning the table that a small stone blue urn with a little ceramic chocolate baby sleeping on top with the words "Our Angel" Jayceon Anthony McCall with his birthday and death date engraved. After a few more minutes, the funeral home's director, who was officiating the service, started the eulogy for my nephew.

"Now I've only been knowing Ms. Nguyen here a few days now and let me tell y'all, she's the sweetest gal ever. I'm sure all of y'all know that already though. When she came in here, she looked defeated and told me how she had just done this for her own mother a few months prior. I prayed with her and told her that God gives his strongest soldiers the toughest battles. I am here to tell all of y'all the battles we face everyday are just trials. There cannot be a testimony with a test. Jayceon may have not been able to make it into y'all's lives, but know that God has a plan for his mother. Even in death, he is with you. You carried him for eight and a half months and had him on earth for only twenty days, but he knew his mama loved him. The Lord also surrounded Dasiah with the love and support she needed at this time."

I squeezed her hand as he continued.

"Even though baby Jayceon has gone on to be with our father God, he is forever in our hearts. I pray God has mercy on the soul that caused distress to this innocent soul and that his mother finds comfort in knowing she had the pleasure of carrying him. Let's us pray." He said as I watched him bow his head and closed his eyes. I followed suit as I listened to the prayer asking for comfort and understanding and also giving great vibes to my sister. He prayed for the future and ended the prayer. When we all looked up, all you could hear were soft sniffles coming from all over the small chapel. I wiped the tears that slowly streamed down my face. Dasiah sat next to me quietly weeping as Lil handed her a tissue to wipe her eyes. I real deal hated seeing my sister like this, and I hated we hadn't gotten to fully experience my nephew. Glee was softly rubbing my leg as the director concluded the service.

Glee excused himself to take a call, and Dasiah and Khalil went up to accept the urn and speak with the director. I took this as my opportunity to go speak to Raph. I found him still near the pew he was sitting in, talking with someone else who had come. He saw me approaching and ended his conversation and the guy he was talking to walked off.

"Lil mama, man I'm sorry y'all going through all this." Raph said. giving me a brotherly hug.

"Thank you Raph. You know my sister and I appreciate it." I said.

"So y'all leaving soon or what?" Raph asked.

As I explained that I'd be heading home the following day and that Dasiah would be leaving in a week, Raph listened as my eyes met a now angry Glee. He was headed over to where Dasiah and Lil was, never breaking his death stare he was giving me.

Raph picked up on my facial changes and spoke cautiously.

"Niya, everything good? Have I done something wrong?" He asked with concern.

I wanted to be honest with Raph because I cared enough about him to spare him from the wrath of Glee. While I had never seen Glee upset to the point he did something, I didn't want to test him. Just as I was about to answer him, I felt someone's presence approaching. When I turned around, it was Dasiah coming over. She stepped around me to hug Raph.

"Thank you so much for coming Raphael. If it wasn't for you, this might have been a double funeral." Dasiah said sadly.

" I'm just glad I was able to help you. I am sorry about your seed though. Shit fucked up."

I looked behind me as Khalil and Glee watched us intensely. Lil looked neutral as I could see Glee whisper to him. I turned my attention back to my sister and Raph's conversation. I listened as Dasiah promised Raph she'd stop by before leaving, and I took the time to say my goodbyes now because I already knew Glee was going to cuss my black ass out. I was mentally preparing for it. Raph and I shared one last hug before Dasiah and I went to join the boys. As we approached, Glee was already on the dumb shit by ignoring me. When I walked up close to him, he quickly stepped back. Dasiah caught the petty gesture towards me, sucking her teeth and shooting him a dirty look. Jayceon's tiny final resting place was sitting on the pew they had been standing next to. I watched my sister pick up the urn in one swift motion.

"Come on baby sister. Let's go get a bottle and drink at home."

She said, cutting her eyes at Lil before linking her arm with mine and leading us out of the chapel. We walked over to her car and got in as she secured the urn in the back seat. After making sure it wouldn't move with the makeshift barrier she had made with a couple jackets and double assuring it didn't move by putting the seat belt on, we took off towards a liquor store. My sister was well aware that I wasn't a big drinker. I mean our mama had given me a couple sips of her wine coolers when I was younger and those taste like juice to me. I just couldn't taste the lil five percent of alcohol they claimed was in it. Unlike most teenagers, I wasn't into drinking. I didn't like how I felt while under the influence of alcohol and opted to smoke because I like the euphoric feeling it gave me. Nevertheless, if my sister wanted to have a drink, I was going to participate because she needed me.

We pulled into an ABC liquor store and Dasiah ran in and grabbed a bottle of Seagrams gin. She navigated back to her apartment complex. She carried the drink while I retrieved the urn. Looking around the semi-empty parking lot, I didn't see Glee's Mercedes anywhere. That indicated Daish and I would be nice and toasty when they did arrive. We went upstairs and Dasiah grabbed the urn from me and made her way to the stand near her television. She placed the small urn on the shelf before returning to the kitchen to make our drinks. She mixed the gin, orange juice, and Sprite then used her shaker to mix it all together. Once she had filled our stemless glasses, she turned on the five disc CD player stereo she had as Brandy's voice filled the space. She skipped the Intro and went to as she retrieved a pre-rolled blunt off the table and sparked it up.

I would usually babysit the fuck out of a drink but the way Glee had me feeling, compelled me to drink. I downed the alcoholic beverage effortlessly as if I was frequent drinker, but those around me knew otherwise. When I sat the empty glass down, Dasiah was looking at me crazy.

"Damn sis, you want another one?" She asked with a chuckle.

Without a second thought, I shook my head yes and she got up and made me another one. Before I knew it, I had no control of my laughter, my legs, or my thoughts. Between the five and a half drinks I had chugged down and the three blunts we had smoked, I was fucked up. The boys still hadn't made it home, and I no longer cared how Glee was feeling. Dasiah had told me that she wasn't feeling how Glee had reacted to Raph and I couldn't agree more. How did he expect me to be in a relationship with him if he was going to be insecure? Glee was the first dude I was actually interested in, and I didn't want my first real relationship experience to be what it was becoming. I let out a sigh as we vibed out to Mariah Carey's album Rainbow. Dasiah was singing along to "Petals" like she had set in on Mariah's studio session. I remembered when I was younger, Dasiah would always walk around the house singing songs by Whitney and Mariah. I would like listening to her sing, and while Dasiah would argue she could only carry a tune, she actually had a pretty singing voice.

I closed my eyes and let my sister's voice aid in soothing me as the song came to an end. I stayed up with Dasiah a little while longer until I couldn't keep my eyes open. Given my head was spinning, the only thing that made me feel better was closing my eyes. I opened my eyes long enough to see that Dasiah had fallen asleep curled up on the small loveseat. I managed to get up but not before I fell down twice, struggling to find my balance. When I successfully had my footing, I stumbled all the way back to the room, bracing myself using the walls. When I made it to the room, I fought with myself as I tried taking off my clothes. After five minutes of trying to get the dress off, I finally was pulling it over my head. I slung it over by where my bags were and climbed in the bed in my matching bra and panty set. As soon as my head hit the pillow, I was out.

|Khalil|

Glee was still feeling salty about Daniya and Raph's interaction at the memorial earlier. Even after knowing the situation, my dawg was not letting up on the fact that his lady was in another nigga's face. I was sitting across from him at Wing House, enjoying an order of buffalo wings and a basket of fries. He was playing over his food and the shit was starting to really annoy me. I had to remember that Glee was younger than me sometimes, so when he got like this, he reminded me of a lil ass boy. I never spared my lil nigga though, so I was about to talk some sense into the nigga before they took off back home tomorrow.

"Dawg you know you trippin' right?" I said, dunking a couple fries into the pile of ketchup I had on my plate.

"Man, Ion hear none of dat shit you talking bruh. I feel like she trying me. I specifically asked her to not be in that nigga's face." Glee said through gritted teeth.

I looked at this nigga like he had two heads. Was he listening to what he was saying?

"You do know this the same nigga that made sure Dasiah made it to the hospital? He wanna fuck Jordan up just as much as we do." I said, trying to reason with him. It appeared he was thinking about what I had just said, but no sooner than his face displayed a look of consideration, it turned back sour.

"Nah man... he want my bitch." Glee said, finally taking a real bite of the barbeque wings he had gotten. Sometimes I wondered as old as Glee portrayed himself to be, did he realize he was still a kid at nineteen. I remember being exactly like him at that age, but I had Dasiah to balance me out. Given Glee had only been fucking around with hoes and not committing to them, this was his first real relationship.

"Nigga do you hear yourself? That man don't want Niya... you trippin' forreal. Plus Niya would never do anything to jeopardize what y'all got." I said, hoping to persuade my protégé.

"If she wouldn't jeopardize us, then her ass would have done what I asked and steered clear of that nigga." Glee said with aggravation and anger laced in his voice.

I shook my head at how stubborn this nigga was being. While him and his lil boo boo were beefing, I had been heavily entertaining the idea of me and Daish rekindling. I wanted my old thang back. I had been debating within myself and while my old ways weren't completely gone, I refused to allow our past issues be the reason I didn't see what really could become of her and I. She had always been my rider and had held a nigga down countless times.

I didn't know what to say to my boy, but I needed him to tighten up on his feelings because I didn't need my ex-girl, who was set to be my next girl, mad at me because he was mad at her kid sister. I wanted them to work out, but if that meant my girl was going to punish me every time they went through something, then maybe they didn't need to be together.

"My guy listen, you won't know if she is for you if you keep your foot on her neck. Give her the rope to hang herself, and if for some reason she never does and she proves she's a rider, then you should never have to question her. Shit y'all been doing business together this long, has she ever made you question her loyalty?" I inquired, waiting to hear the obvious answer. Had she shown disloyalty, he wouldn't be trying to tie her ass down.

"Nah never." He said, stroking his goatee.

"See man, let her breathe... time will show and prove." I said, signaling to the waitress to bring our check.

We finished our late lunch and were headed back to the apartment until Glee made a detour. I hoped this nigga was preparing to make it up to Niya. As if he could read my mind, he pulled into the twenty four hour Walgreens on International Speedway. He damn near double parked as he grabbed a spot near the entrance.

"Nigga you better grab something nice. Yo ass was trippin'."

He chuckled as we both exited the vehicle and entered the well known drugstore brand. I watched as Glee headed towards the candy aisle. He spent about ten minutes browsing the plethora of candy options. I saw him grab several different types of gummy candy before heading towards the card aisle. He browsed a selection of cheesy cards but settled on a black card with a happy African American couple on front. Next, he headed to the freezer section and grabbed a Snickers ice cream and proceeded to head to the register. I was walking behind him but staring at a text from Tai. Shawty had been hitting my line, but I always managed to miss it or I just plain ignored it. I mean don't get me wrong ,Tai was an awesome girl and had a lot of potential, but she was not for me. Dasiah would always have my heart and until I tried this second time around, I wasn't interested. I shoved my phone back in my pocket as I waited for Glee to finish paying for his purchases before we headed back to his car.

"Nigga you better hope this shit make her feel better because I'm sure Dasiah and her are probably still sitting up mad."

"Nigga if this don't work, Ion even know what Ima do." Glee said, driving out the nearly deserted parking lot.

As we drove back to the crib, Big Tymers' *Millionaire Dream* blared out of the speaker. Glee automatically joined in.

♫ **"Ridin' to myself up in my baby Benz**

Playin' tens, goin' shoppin' with my lady friends

Flyin' to Nashville, me and bob splittin' eighty

Then I chill on Washatona with Slim and Baby

See the $ on my back symbolize my click

See the $ around my neck symbolize we rich." ♫

We both vibed out as we maneuvered through the streets headed back to the complex. Earlier at the memorial, Glee told me that Tez had cleaned up the lil mess we had going on back at home. When he told me Lil Face had been snooping around the trap for Keno's stupid ass, I knew that I needed to get rid of that lame ass nigga. After instructing Tez to move our spot and off Lil Face, it was only a matter of time before that fuck nigga Keno figured out we were on to him. While he was trying to get one up on us, we were already ten steps ahead of his slow ass. I knew that Glee had this low-key party planned for Daniya's birthday, and by the time Daish and I had tied up her loose ends here, we would be back just in time for the turn up. As we pulled into the complex, most of the parking lot was filled from the normal residents and Glee had to find a parking spot in the next building. Once he locked his whip and had set the alarm, we made our way up to the second floor apartment that had been home for me for past few weeks.

I used the key Daish had given me to get inside and my eyes landed on a sleeping Daish with an empty bottle of gin on the coffee table, and I knew her ass couldn't have drunk the entire bottle. Glee was scanning the apartment just like me because Niya was nowhere to be found. He proceeded down the hall while I picked up a sleeping Dasiah and carried her to her room. As I tucked her in and made sure she was straight, I just stared at her for a minute before shutting her door and retreating back to the living room. It had been a long day.

|Glee|

I had heard my big homie loud and clear. Maybe I had been trippin' on Niya, but this relationship shit was new to me. I was used to spending money on a bitch, smashing, and moving along, but with Niya, she had never had her hand out. She had actually asked me to help her make her own money, and while I had been apprehensive about having a female running plays for me, she had proven she was more than capable of doing so. Her loyalty had never been in question, and I was making myself look like a pure asshole. When I opened the door to the room, I found Niya knocked the fuck out. I knew she was drunk because I could smell the alcohol permeating off of her. I sat down the bag of goodies I had for her and went over and kissed her on the lips. I could taste the gin on her lips as I moved away from her. I knew now who had drunk most of that bottle. I suddenly remembered the Snicker ice cream I had purchased and ran to put it in the freezer. Returning back to the room, I wasn't prepared to pull the covers back and find Niya in just her bra and panties. I was so tempted to pull them off and feast on her, but I needed her to be awake when I pleasured her.

I removed my shoes, Polo slacks, and my shirt, paying close attention to not wake Niya. I snuggled up close to her, wrapping my arms around her, attempting to get comfortable. I felt shitty about how I had done her, and I didn't want to get on the road the following day with bad blood. My baby birthday was coming up, and I wanted it to be special for her. It had been a tough year for her thus far, and I wanted it to end on a good note. When we got back in the city, it would be crunch time to make sure that the surprise party I had planned went off without a hitch. I could feel my nature rising, but I was still trying to respect Dasiah's spot. I had been deprived and while a drunk Niya probably would have been fun, I knew she had gone to bed mad at a nigga, so the last thing she probably wanted was for me to touch her. I laid up for an hour or so before I allowed myself to sleep for a few hours.

|Jordan|

I got word that today was Jayceon's memorial. There was a small handful of people that don't believe that I beat Dasiah. They just can't see me acting in that manner, and even though I know what I did, I appreciated the small support I still had on campus. I had opted to take my last couple credits online to avoid running into any trouble. I knew my parents, my mother in particular, would be calling soon to check on Dasiah and inquiring about her grandchild. I wouldn't be able to give her an answer, so my plan was to avoid her and my dad's calls as long as I could. I wasn't surprised that Dasiah hadn't extended an invite to Jayceon's memorial service. After our last encounter at the hospital, I pretty much knew where I stood with her and that thug she chose to associate herself with. While I would always have some love for her, I knew that we would never be anything ever again. Jayceon's death ended everything between us.

Candice had been keeping herself on my mind, and I was happy to wake up to a good morning text from her on the daily. Jordan was released yesterday and was his usual annoying self. He thought because his ass was injured that I was going to be catering to his every beckoning call. He was in for a rude awakening, especially since his ass was in this predicament because of his own damn self. As I was getting closer with Candice, I hoped that all this talk time she was giving me would lead to something more solid. I planned on taking her out on a proper date just as soon as I tied up my loose ends with my course work and then I could really see where this thing was going.

I was in the bedroom enjoying the bed to myself. Daylen's injury had been a gift and a curse. Besides having to look out for him, I could actually get a good night worth of sleep. I had been enjoying the one day and hoped I had a few more alone. I don't know why but I started to feel this disconnect from him. While I honestly had never seen us settling down, I knew I couldn't give him what he was looking for. I loved Daylen for his supportive nature, but I wasn't in love with him. I knew no matter how I said it or showed him I was done, he would never accept that things between us had run their course. I listened to the crickets as they made the still night seem so busy with their repetitive noises that they made.

I had been scratching one particular spot on my arm for over a week now, and I was sure my eczema that I had been dealing with since my junior year of high school was flaring up. It was so hard to not scratch, and once I started in the triggered area, I had an uncontrollable itch in other places, so I would scratch them as well. The shit had started to get annoying, and I was going to have to have my mom schedule me an appointment with a dermatologist. I thought I had maintained it all these years by switching to sensitive skin products, but it seemed to be back. I made a mental note to call my mom later to set up an appointment for me. I was tired of the uncontrollable itching I was experiencing. Not to mention, I was feeling rather fatigued and hadn't changed much in my lifestyle. It was time for a check-up and a much needed break from Daytona Beach.

Chapter 7

|Dasiah|

As Khalil and I stood in the complex parking lot waving goodbye to my sister and Glee, it was a bittersweet moment. Given the reason they were even here made it bitter, but we'd be back in the 727 in a few days so that made it sweet. Glee had confided in us about the surprise party he had planned, and I couldn't contain the excitement I felt for my baby sister. Given she had suffered as a child more than me because of the absence of her father made it that more important that our mama had raised us to never rely on a man. It wasn't a shock to me that Niya had turned to the streets for her income. It was better than her either being a stripper or a prostitute. While she was aiding in the volunteer poisoning of our community, pill heads were mostly white people, so I didn't have sympathy for them in that essence. They were the ones that got addicted to pills; black people got addicted to crack. While it was a stereotypical thought, it was true.

Khalil followed close behind me as we made our way back up to my apartment. In the next few days, I would be breaking my lease all thanks to Lil, and we too would be hitting the road. I had dropped out of the last few classes I had, and I wasn't sure when I'd be going back to school, but I would be going back one day. Like clockwork, Lil sparked up a phat ass blunt he had rolled prior to Niya and Glee leaving, and we both plopped down on the couch to encourage it. I admired him as he inhaled and exhaled the loud blunt smoke. I had always admired his full succulent lips; me and Shayna used to say he had pussy eating lips. And once he and I started messing around, it was apparent that he had some lips made especially for eating the box. His lips hid a set of the most perfect set of teeth and whether he was smiling or gritting them, he was fine. He kept his hair cut low and brushed his waves religiously. I had always joked with Shayna about us making babies and them being damn near blind because of my chinky eyes and Khalil's almond shaped eyes.

Sitting here admiring the man I thought I'd spend the rest of my life with had me also reminiscing on my friend. The day she died, a piece of me left with her. I knew Khalil had been going back and forth with Keno, and while he hadn't fired the shot that killed her, he had participated in the careless shootout that had taken her life at only sixteen, it still haunted me. Shayna had been the life of the party and had it not been for her, Khalil and I would have never gotten together. I know had she still been alive when I first found out I was pregnant with Khalil's baby that she would have made me go against my mother. And had my mom kicked me out, Shayna would have moved me in with her and her grandmother no questions asked. She had been a real ride or die friend and for some reason, I felt like I had failed her. I think all the time about her making it and the bullet missing, but then I probably wouldn't have signed up for school; and even though right now hindsight was twenty twenty, I was now a college dropout. I knew my friend was looking down on me smiling as she and my mama traded off holding Jayceon. I had three guardian angels looking out for me.

Lil nudging me brought me back to reality. I had almost forgotten he was sitting right next to me. I shook the urge to cry as I took the blunt he was handing to me.

"Yo ass wasn't even listening." He said.

Even though I had not, I acted as if I had been.

"Yes huh." I said with a coy smile.

"Then what I said then?" He challenged.

I had no fucking idea what he had said, and I couldn't keep up the charade long. I sucked my teeth before busting out in laughter.

"Man... Ion know what you said, damn!" I confessed.

"Exactly! Don't never be listening to a nigga... let a nigga mention shopping or some shit, you all ears." He retorted with a smirk attached.

I couldn't help that I had the attention span of a hamster and oftentimes found myself zone out.

"What did you say Lil? I'm sorry, I just was thinking about something." I said, hitting the blunt and holding the potent loud in my chest.

He looked over at me while fidgeting with his hands. When Khalil fidgeted, it was usually something serious he wanted to discuss. I hit the blunt for a couple seconds before passing it back to him in hopes it would motivate him to get whatever it was off his chest. He took the lit blunt and took a few pulls from it before speaking.

"Daish, baby…" He began but his phone vibrating in his pocket broke him away for only a second. He looked at whomever that was calling and slid his phone back in his pocket. I thought nothing of it as he picked back up with what he was saying.

"The time we been spending together, while it hasn't been for the best reasons, those reasons have helped me realize that I'd rather go through more ups than downs with you. You have always been my wifey, my future, my Bonnie.

You know a nigga a gentle thug and shit when it come to my heart, and while you the only person I ever let get close enough to experience this, these last few weeks have shown me that you the only one I want near my heart, body, and soul. You have always completed me baby. And I apologize for giving you away girl. Seem like had I been thinking like a man and less like a boy, you wouldn't have gone through half the shit you been going through. I guess what I'm trying to say is or ask rather is will you give a nigga another chance?" He hit the blunt so coolly after getting that off his chest that it hadn't even seemed like he had just poured his heart out to me.

It was crazy how Lil had just thrown all that at me at once. Yet with all the things I had on my mind, this had to be the best thing all week. The man I had loved since I was fifteen was re-professing his love for me. I knew my answer already, it was clear as crystal. I did something I had been dying to do since we had made it back to my apartment, but given the circumstances, I didn't want to make it weird between us. His plea for us to be together again just solidified what I was preparing myself for. As I threw my mid back length hair in a ponytail, I dropped down to my knees to confirm his answer and to satisfy a longing I had been having since the moment he came to my rescue. I got his eight and a half inch even toned dick out in one motion since he had on basketball shorts, and before he could protest, I went to town sucking his dick. He nearly dropped the blunt before putting it out himself. I controlled my breathing and did all the shit I remembered he liked. The slow tongue action I was giving the tip of his dick had Lil staring me dead in my eyes as our souls realigned.

I didn't care if my eyes popped out of their sockets. I had a personal point to prove to him. Plus, I had been missing him and his dick, I mean my dick. He was into my head game and had always been. I was able to make his eyes roll in the back of his head when I hit him with the vacuum seal double hand twist gawk gawk 3000. This always made this nigga bust quick and I was definitely planning on riding his face and dick when I was done. As I felt his dick stiffen in my mouth, I prepared for his first load. I planned on sucking and fucking him dry for the rest of the day. We were about to make up for old times.

Six Days Later

|Alani|

Seeing that circled date one day away had me happy as fuck. I would finally be able to get my revenge on Niya for trying to stunt on me a while back. She might have thought she had beaten my ass outside the trap for the world to see, and while I had gone home with my tail between my legs defeated, I knew that when the time had come for me to get my get back, I would be the one getting the last laugh. While I had been replaying how I was going to stomp the shit out of Niya on her birthday, I had also been preparing myself for my impromptu entrance to the party she didn't even know about. Most of the block had been invited, even though Glee and Niya had been supposedly in Daytona Beach after her sister lost her baby or some shit, so no one could ruin the surprise. Had the raggedy bitch been round here, I would have ruined the lil surprise in more than one way. I was determined to make that lil nappy headed bitch pay.

I was staring in my closet at ten o'clock in the morning, looking at the perfect outfit to crash a party in. I had been doing a helluva lot of hair to afford the outfit I was calling my revenge fit. It was a see through catsuit with sequins covering my titties and pussy area; my ass was the only thing you could see. I was going to wand curl my hair and do some light makeup. I had gotten some crystal encrusted Giuseppe's especially for the occasion. I hated to have to fight in the catsuit, but Niya had to give me, me. Glee would get to see this ass one last time before I quit his ass for good. After he saw how I mopped the floor with his lil basic bitch, he was going to wish he had of acted right. I sparked up one of three blunts I had rolled as I prepped for my lazy day. I would be spending the rest of my day relaxing and retaining my energy.

|Glee|

My radio blasted the most appropriate song for this moment. As I looked over at my beautiful girlfriend of officially a week, Tupac's *Me and My Girlfriend* flowed out my car speakers like it was made to be played specifically from my whip. I was holding Niya's left hand with my right as I used my left hand to navigate through the city. Niya had set up a hair appointment across town, and while I much rather she find an equally talented chicken head on our side of town, this girl was supposedly one of the best in the city. If Niya wanted to go to the best then Niya went to the best. I wasn't short changin' for nothin' or nobody when it came to my lil baby. I lifted her hand up and brought it to my lips and placed a delicate kiss on it, lingering the kiss. I looked up at her as she smiled a big ol' grin at me. I was really feeling her. While Daytona had tested me a lil, it was a small thing to a giant. Niya and I had an entire four hours to talk on the way home, and I was man enough to apologize for my childish ass behavior. She hadn't deserved that shit, and I had been diligently working on being a better man. Plus the bag full of Gummy's and the Hallmark Expressions card added the cherry on top.

"Baby what we doing tomorrow?" She asked, intertwining her fingers with mine.

"I keep telling yo ass wait till tomorrow." I said with a smirk.

Since we had gotten back home on Saturday, Niya had been inquiring about her birthday. I gave her the same response "wait until your birthday." I didn't want her knowing shit, not even a hint. While a few people knew about the party, I knew they would never tell Niya. Had her and Alani still been cool, I knew her ass would have spilled the beans just to be spiteful. I can't believe I ever put my dick in her. Bev Biv Devoe said "you shouldn't trust a big butt and a smile," but I think they had missed them light eyed mu'fuckas too. I was glad I had Niya sexually and as a business partner. While Lil would forever be my big bruh, I now had someone I could run the world with, and she wasn't like anything I was used to. I had my eyes on the road but just thinking about her drove me crazy. I made my way cross Thirty Fourth and a short time later, we arrived at the shop she was getting her hair done. I gave her a peck on the lips before watching her walk in the shop.

****

Tez had the biggest of Daniya's gifts ducked off for me. I had to put the finishing touches to it, but it would be ready to shit on anything that parked near it. My baby was going to love the 2001 Lexus RX that I got for her. It was magenta with chrome accents and her street name carved in the head rests. The car was definitely gone draw haters to my baby. If a fuck nigga doubted if we were eating over here, this would let it be known that we were eating like kings cross Ninth. I was outside our new dope spot, which was actually better than the last because we actually could pull in the back of the house, and there was a durable privacy fence easily secluding our illegal activities. Tez was servin' a fiend on the side of the house as I sat in my whip and counted the five bands I was setting aside for my errands. I still needed to grab food, drank, and of course we had bud, so the party was going to be off the chain. I was having the party at the Masonic Hall, besides the limited parking the venue was nice. Some of the biggest parties happened there too, so I was hoping for a great turn out, and I also hoped these mu'fuckas knew how to behave.

After chopping it up with Tez for what seemed like an hour until his babymama showed up to snatch him off the block for a lil, I maintained my post at the spot as buddies kept coming for their fix. I knew Niya would shoot me a text or call when she was ready. She had already warned me that her hair wasn't something that could be just thrown together. She was getting a sew-in and that shit could take a few hours to achieve the look she was going for. That was fine by me because it meant I could make some of my money back that I had already dished out. I never got tired of making money, but I really could use a vacation from the streets. As the day unwind more and my pockets begin to grow, I got the text I had been waiting for. My baby was ready!

|Khalil|

Watching Daish trying to wiggle her slim thick ass in these jeans was quite amusing. Had I not known that she had a lil ass back there, I would have sworn that I had just gave her this ass after our four day sexual romp. We had spent the time reacquainting ourselves in more ways than one. We had gotten to my condo on St. Pete Beach a few hours ago, and Dasiah wanted to make it to see the sunset. It had been something else we had memories doing together, but this time around, neither of us would take it for granted. I was just admiring her for her tenacity. She was going through so much but had managed to brighten up my life. I swore I was going to do right by her. God rest Ms. Kandi's soul because this time around, if I skeeted in this, she was having each and every one of my kids.

"Baby hurry up! We gone miss the sunset!" I joked, poking light fun at the fact that she always said that when we were running late, but right now in this moment, she was in fact the late one. I laughed as she playfully cut her eyes at me.

"Baby you think I got too much stuff?" She asked, looking around the bedroom at all her unpacked items from Daytona. She had packed outfits in a separate duffle and was living out of the bag for now.

"Nah babe, you just getting here. I didn't expect you to have it out the way in a day. Long as we can get to the bed, I'm straight" I honestly said.

She batted her eyes my way followed by her Colgate smile and it's like my dick just reacts. Those two things along made me want her off her looks. She looked exotic as fuck to me all those years ago and with time, she had aged even better at twenty.

"I'm ready Lil... let's go before I miss it." She said, snatching her clutch and phone off the counter as we headed out to make new memories from old ones.

****

Six Hours Later

"Bro why you just ain't tell the girl to beat it man? I feel bad about that ass whoopin' my sister just gave her." Niya said as she doubled over in laughter.

Hell I was feeling bad for Tai too. Dasiah must have taken out all her pent up frustrations on the poor girl because she had just worn that ass whoopin'. I had been avoiding her calls for a reason, but it didn't stop Ms. Tai from stopping by my place unannounced. I just thought if someone stopped answering or hitting you up, it was universal for they weren't interested. I guess she hadn't gotten the memo and had paid the price when Dasiah walked in with Niya a few moments ago.

The fight had only lasted long enough for Daish to sock Tai in her eye and pull a few tracks out. I knew my baby was a scrapper, but she should have been a boxer the way she threw punches. Tai ran up outta here with empty threats and tears running down her face, but I knew if she hadn't learned anything today, she had learned to call before she came. When she invited herself in, I tried so hard to push her ass back out the door; but shawty had never done anything to me, so I opted to listen to her. But when she started talking about her and me being a thing, I had to remind her that we had just been fucking round but that was going to be ending because I was back with my ex. When she decided that she wouldn't take no for an answer, Tai tried throwing that pussy on a nigga but not fast enough because my lady was on her ass like a spider monkey. Daish knew me like the back of her hand, and when I was committed, I was loyal than a dog to its master.

"Damn sis... Happy Birthday!" I said, finally acknowledging the first two hours of Niya's birthday.

"Aww thanks brother." She said with a smile as she pulled out a blunt and proceeded to light it.

"Turn up then!" Daish resurfaced from the back.

"Babe, I advise you tell your old hoes that wifey's back and ain't gone be no more poppin' up over here or nowhere for that matter." Dasiah said, coming over and sitting on my lap.

"I'm so happy for y'all." Niya gushed over our renewed love.

"I'm glad everything is finally looking up for all of us. I know it's been rough on y'all." I said, taking my own blunt out.

"I wished my boo was here." Niya said, looking sad briefly.

I knew my dawg was making sure tomorrow went off without a hitch. He had already sent me a few pictures of the set up and the shit was fly. He had really went out for Niya's sixteenth birthday. All he asked of us was that we kept Niya away for a lil, so he could tie up his loose ends. We took a couple birthday shots of gin with Niya, and before we knew it, she was passed out on the couch. Dasiah covered her up and we both went to the back to my room to crash.

Chapter 8

|Daylen|

Jordan had really been smelling himself lately. If he thought I didn't know about that ol' polly pocket head ass bitch he was entertaining from McDonald's, he was in for a rude awakening. I already had sights on that bitch, and I was feeling like my messy petty self again. I was tired of playing these games with Jordan, and while he couldn't live in his truth, I was about to live mine and nothing but the truth was about to escape my lips. I had been on AOL messenger and had gained the girl Candice's information from a friend of a friend. Anybody that knew my petty ass knew I kept some friends of friends in the clutch. When I let ol' girl know what was what, I knew she was going to pump the brakes on anything she thought they were going to be doing. I was sipping some pink lemonade, still lounging on the couch when I hit the send button. I laughed to myself as I waited for a response.

I heard that lil Asian bitch paid her last respects to her son last week. Jordan was dead ass wrong for putting that girl through that, but I had no remorse for her ass. She better hoped she didn't have what we had. I knew Jordan had it, and he didn't have a clue what was going on with his body. I had noticed the rash weeks ago, and I smiled every time he scratched at it. I knew he probably thought his parents could just pay some money and this would go away, but I wanted him to wear this death sentence. He was going to pay for making me feel used and abused for the last few years. Had he shown me real love from the moment we started talking, I would have come clean and never touched him; but I had let him in and he had used me for his own personal vices.

The chime from my AIM brought me back.

CandiceW81: Who is this?

DayDay69: Girl don't worry about it! Did you read my message?

CandiceW81: umm yeah, just a lil confused

DayDay69: Girl you ain't no damn confused. Either you fucking the nigga or you ain't!

CandiceW81: ....

Before she could respond, I dropped the bomb on her ass.

DayDay69: Well if you is giving him the cat, that pussy infected! That nigga got HIV.

CandiceW81: :O

DayDay69: ;)

CandiceW81: Aim User has logged off

I relished in the fact that the bitch was probably not fucking him, but the fact that she knew now what he didn't even know made me get up off the couch to prepare for the showdown that was bound to happen once he got word.

****

The way Jordan had his forearm pressed against my throat had me slightly turned on but scared. I know it was my fault that our secret was now all over the campus and most of this small as beach city, but I didn't care. I was tired of being such an asset to a nigga that treated me like a liability.

"When were you going to tell me you have HIV?!" Jordan yelled at me with tears and snot running down his face.

I was trying so hard not to smile, but I couldn't help it. This had been the reaction I had longed for from him. I wanted all this passion behind something other than a bitch.

"Shit, why should I have told you?!" I spat back.

I saw the rage in his eyes, and I also saw sadness. That was something I hadn't prepared myself to see. While I had been selfishly passing on something that had been given to me in the same manner, I had always said I didn't want anyone to feel what I was feeling, but here I was being confronted for doing the very thing I had been against. I was no better than the man who gave it to me. For the first time since exposing him to Candice, I felt bad. I had ruined a life, but to me, he had ruined me. Jordan must have forgotten I was a man because he wasn't about to do me how he had done Dasiah. I pushed him off me as I drew back and punched him as hard as I could. He immediately grabbed his nose, but instinctively, he squared up to fight. I ran my ass to my knife block and pulled out the biggest butcher's knife it held. I flailed about with the knife in my hand, trying to keep Jordan away from me. He wasn't letting up though as he chased me around my living room.

I had forgotten about my injury and was now feeling my adrenaline running low as the pain kicked in. I doubled over in pain and in the midst of nursing my wound, Jordan was able to get the butcher knife from me. I was now squatting on the floor, pleading for him to let me go.

"Please... I'm sorry... I never meant..." As I attempted to finish my statement, Jordan carelessly stabbed me multiple times in the chest then he crouched down and whispered,

"I'll see you in hell!" He slit my throat in one swift move. As life left my body, I hoped we'd meet at hell's gates together.

|Jordan|

I-95 wasn't as slammed as I thought as I made my way to my parent's house. Killing Daylen had brought me so much satisfaction because he had me all the way fucked up. Since he liked to play with knives, it was only fitting that I took his faggot ass out with one. While my intentions weren't to kill him when I arrived, him introducing the knife into our fight had triggered the thought. Earlier when Candice started sending me rapid fire texts about being a dirty ass dog and a walking infestation, I was beyond confused. I was floored when she finally picked up the phone and damn near yelled that someone had reached out to her saying "I had HIV." When she told me how she had gotten an AIM notification from a user named DayDay69, I knew exactly who had messaged her and my blood instantly started boiling. Why was someone I barely knew but liked telling me something about myself that I didn't know? The person I had been dealing with for the past three years had negated the fact that he was infected with such a permanent infection. I could kick my own ass for being so careless.

I was driving the best of my ability, given I was trying to drive with tears stinging my eye.s Every time I wiped my eyes, more would just pour out. How had I been so reckless to believe that something of this magnitude couldn't happen to me? I wanted this to be a dream. No, I needed it to be a dream. I couldn't believe how much of Daylen's blood was covering my clothing. Fuccck! I exclaimed out loud to no one but me. I felt even more alone in this world. HIV?! How the fuck was I going to deal with such a finite diagnosis?

****

The letter I was writing would explain everything: the death of Jayceon, the ending of Dasiah's and my relationship, and a host of other hidden issues I had been hiding from my parents. I had never thought about suicide so much than I had driving home. It seemed like the most plausible solution. I wasn't living for anything now. My dreams of being a world renowned scientist were out the window. Everything that I had worked so hard for was no longer an option. As I finished the letter, my father's snub nose .38 Smith & Wesson was in my direct line of sight. I had grabbed it from my father's office desk drawer when I arrived. While I was going to end my life upon it touching my hand, I had enough sense to not leave my parents questioning anything. I had no proof that I was indeed infected, but the rash I had was turning into lesions all over.

I knew something wasn't right, and I couldn't bare living with all the shit I'd allowed to happen.

I placed the barrel of the pistol in my mouth and pulled the trigger, hoping my parents understood and was ready to fight Daylen for eternity.

|Daniya|

Glee had the Masonic Hall decked the fuck out. I was finally sixteen and the shit felt like it had taken forever for my birthday to come. I had on an all white deep V ladder open back slinky bodycon dress with a pair of peep toe iridescent pumps from Steve Madden. The dress hugged these sixteen year old curves perfectly and the heels gave my calf muscles a front row look at all the action. My hair was laid and the hairstylist had done her damn thing. Glee's eyes lit up when I stepped out the car when he came to pick me up and mine had done the same when I saw the magenta and silver color scheme he had chosen for this party. I mean I wasn't expecting all this, but a girl was floored. We had only been official for a week, but he had shown me in more ways than one that he was with me.

Everybody who fucked with Glee and I was in the building. I felt the love flowing throughout the building. When I spotted my sister walking over with a pink wrapped gift, I got hype.

"Wassup baby sister?! You like your surprise?" She said with a huge grin on her face as she handed the gift to me. I would open it up with the rest of my presents later. As I accepted the gift, Ludacris's hit *What's Your Fantasy* came out hard and bangin' through the DJ's speakers.

♫ "I wanna, li-li-li-lick you from your head to your toes

And I wanna, move from the bed down to the, down to the, to the flo'

Then I wanna, "Ahh ahh," you make it so good I don't wanna leave

But I gotta kn-kn-kn-know, what-what's your fan-ta-ta-sy?" ♫

Everybody was on the dance floor dancing and rapping. I had never felt so much love for me in one place. I looked over and my entire face flipped upside down.

"What the fuck that hoe doing here?" Daish asked on the side of me as we both watched Alani walk in with a sparkly catsuit on. Ohh this hoe tried to come here and steal my shine! I saw Glee approach her as she put her hand up in his face. He quickly sideswiped her hand out his face, but after the third time of him doing it, I stormed over to where they were.

"Bitch why yo ass here?!" I yelled at her over the music.

"Oh bitch you thought I'd miss my bestie's sixteen birthday?" She said with a grin.

Before I knew it, she had snuck a quick punch in, but I ate that shit, stumbling back right into Dasiah. Before I knew it, my sister was working that hoe with a left hook, then a right hook, followed by an uppercut, and then a jab. I stepped out of my heels and joined in the assault. She was getting that pressure from both of us. Every time Alani thought she was going to throw a punch, she was blindsided from the direction she wasn't protecting. Lil, Tez, and Glee stood off to the side as we finished whooping this hoe's ass. Once we were done beating the breaks off Alani, Glee and Lil personally carried her out and threw her shit out with her since her shoes were left behind in the scuffle. My sister and I high fived before I stepped back into my shoes.

"Damn sis, if I thought ol' girl at Lil's had gotten an ass whoopin', you just showed me that wasn't shit compared to this one." I said to my sister as she smoothed out her fit.

"Shit these hoes ain't trying me, and they damn sure ain't trying you."

If someone would have told me that Daish's and my relationship would have been like this, I would have told them they were a mu'fuckin' lie. I was so glad that our relationship had improved, and I was looking forward to the upcoming year. As the partygoers started getting back in the party spirit following the incident that just happened, an eerie feeling came over me. As if Glee could read my mind, he came over to check on us with Lil in tow. They both stood with their backs towards the door as I watched a bruised and battered Alani walking back in with Keno right behind her with his gun raised, aiming straight at us. I could hear Dasiah scream Lil's name before the gunfire erupted. Everything happened too fast. I felt Glee shove me before brandishing his gun and letting off rounds in the direction of Keno and Alani. From the spot on the floor where I had been pushed, I could see Tez on the ground unresponsive, and moments later, I saw Alani fall from where she had been standing. I saw Keno turn around and run back out the door with Lil and Glee on his ass. I heard a blood curdling scream escape from one of the people kneeling beside Tez's body; it was his babymama. I knew then that Tez was gone.

|Keno|

I had left my car running when I watched those fuck niggas throw my mu'fuckin' cousin out the party like she was trash. I knew cuzzo had gotten her ass beaten just from how she was limping back to my car. I promptly hopped out, hoping to catch them walking back in. When Alani told me how Daniya and her sister had stomped her ass, that shit was kinda funny, but I knew I needed to air this bitch out for every time Khalil and his lame ass folk had disrespected me. I had Alani lead me in as I saw the lil bitch Daniya make direct eye contact with me. When our eyes locked and I saw that those fuck niggas had they backs to me, I couldn't stop myself from bussin' off quick. In the midst of trying to take one or both them niggas' heads off, I managed to hit that nigga Tez in the neck. He dropped instantly and laid lifeless as shots continued to ring out from both them and me. I hoped my family never found out that I had used my own blood as a human shield, but once the third shot penetrated Alani's body, I let her drop to the ground and took off for my car.

I knew I hadn't hit Khalil or Glee, but Tez was good enough in my book. His death would rock that nigga Lil to his core. I wore a sinister smile on my face as I floored it down Eighteenth back towards my hood. Those niggas weren't going to be after me until they laid that fuck nigga Tez to rest, and I knew that just based off their relationship. That meant I had plenty of time to get the fuck out of dodge before they would be looking to avenge his death.

Chapter 9

One Week Later

|Khalil|

Cortez Miguel Turner had been my nigga since Happy Workers Preschool and while he had never left my side, I had left his. He was one of my main hitters and I had left my nigga unprotected. Those bullets could have hit any one of us, but Tez had been the cost of a beef I should have deaded a long time ago. I regretted now not acting on offing Keno's bitch ass when I first got word he was out. That decision alone would haunt me for the rest of my life. Today, we laid my boy to rest in style. I really thought out of anybody, Tez would grow old with me and still be getting money with me in the years to come, but life had a funny way of showing you that despite what we wanted to happen, we rarely ever got what we wanted. Seeing his mother Ms. Teresa cry made my entire heart shatter. I never wanted anyone to see my mama like that over me, being gun down over no dumb ass shit. Tez was only twenty-three years old and my boy had so much life left in him. His lil girl, Corianna, was about to be one next month and her daddy wasn't going to be there to celebrate it with her. His baby mom's Tiana would have to raise her alone, but I was going to play a major role in baby girl's life.

Dasiah had really been holding shit down for a nigga. If it wasn't for her, I wouldn't have been able to think this last week. Between helping his mom plan his funeral and making sure my right hand Glee was straight, a nigga was mentally exhausted. I hadn't broken down yet because this shit hadn't hit me yet. My nigga was really gone. We were headed back to our condo to change before meeting everybody at the repast at Ms. Teresa's. The service had been sincere and had painted my boy as the man we all knew he was. The news story from that night had painted him as a drug dealing ass thug that had gotten what he deserved. St. Pete news channels had a way of tarnishing a black man's name even in death. Today, we learned my boy was loved by many. Old and young faces came to say goodbye to my boy. Dasiah parked in our designated parking spot and like the mechanical shell I had been all week, I got out. I felt numb... like I couldn't cry, sneeze, laugh, smile, nothin'. Yet strangely, I had been sleeping without struggle, without my usual cat naps. I slept every night this week from the time I laid down from preparing for today to the time I woke up to prepare for today. I had been on an automatic loop for an entire week.

When we finally got into our condo, Daish and I parted ways naturally to get ready to be amongst family and friends. She still hadn't unpacked her things from Daytona, but we had managed to get them out the living room. As I rummaged through my closet, I couldn't help but think about my dawg Tez. I had literally known this nigga since I was three, four years old. His people's knew my peoples. We used to think we were cousins because we were always around each other growing up. We had used the "we cousins" line so many times to fuck some bitches. I chuckled to myself just at how many girls we had ran through before I found my wifey. Thinking about Dasiah, I wanted to smile with glee. She had been going through it this week too, and while her news was delightful to me to an extent, I knew it was just reopening wounds she was trying to move pass. Even in the midst of all we were going through with Tez's death and then her also going through what she was going through, she still managed to be my rock in my darkest hours.

As I settled on a pair of Girbaud jeans, a crispy white tee, and a pair of blindingly white Air Force Ones, I looked at my newest ink job I had done to remember Tez by. It was two hands dappin' up with birds flying off in the sunset with "We Cousins Forever" underneath. I would never forget my boy. We had done a lot in nineteen years, and as long as I had breath in my body, I wasn't going to rest until

Keno also met his final rest. This shit had started out petty, but now it was personal. He had to pay with his life for Tez's life.

|Dasiah|

This past week has been one big clusterfuck after another. When I say Tez's death had rocked us, I meant that shit hit home like Hurricane Andrew. I couldn't take the pain from Lil, nothing that I did or said was going to make Khalil feel better. They had literally been friends since they were fresh out of pull ups. Tez had actually been the one to introduce us to each other and always said "we were destined to be together." I was going to miss his goofy ass. I also got a crazy ass call this week from Mrs. McCall, Jordan's mom. She had told me she had been meaning to call because she hadn't heard much about my due date and was a beginning to get worried; but Jordan had assured her I was on schedule to have Jayceon any day. The horrific scream that poor lady let out when I told her that I had lost the baby and by her own son's hands broke my heart. The next thing that left her mouth floored me. She told me how she and her husband had come home from a business trip and found Jordan dead in his room with a self inflicted gunshot wound. What's worse is that he left a handwritten note telling them everything and then some. Not only did his parents know about his secret lifestyle and him beating me up, he also confessed to murdering Daylen back in Daytona and had also disclosed that he was HIV positive but hadn't been officially tested.

Mrs. McCall told me that they had his body tested and he was in fact HIV positive. She advised me to go get tested and I did. Lil paid for a rapid test, and when the results came back twenty minutes later, we both sighed with relief. I would still have to get another test done in three to four months, but it was worth it when it came to my relationship with Khalil. I knew he was happy Jordan was dead, but he hadn't even spoken on much of it besides asking me what I wanted to do about getting tested. While I was trying to be strong for both Khalil and I, it had been a struggle for me to keep it together. As I slid my feet in my Donna Karan slippers and adjusted my halter top and jean jacket, I rubbed my hands over my rose embroidered pants. I couldn't help but think about what 2001 had in store for us. I knew I didn't want anybody else I loved to die though. I grabbed my purse and met Lil at the door at the same time.

|Daniya|

It took everything in me today to walk up to Tez's casket. While I was the youngin' out the bunch, all these people had watched me grow up. Tez had ran off plenty loose dogs for me as a jit, and I would never be able to thank him again. Glee was still shook up about everything, but he was maintaining. We were headed over to Tez's mama house for a lil bit. I had been trying to get my birthday night out my head since everything happened. I hadn't just seen Tez drop, but Alani had died too. What's fucked up was that Keno had been using her to block the bullets. While we had ended our friendship, I would have never wished death on her. Seeing her lifeless body had put a permanent image forever etched in my memories of her stone cold eyes looking through me. This had been my worst birthday ever.

Out of all the gifts I had received, the magenta and chrome Lexus truck with "Lil Mama" stitched in the headrest would have stolen the show, but due to the circumstances of that night, I never got my truck as intended. Glee told me that he had parked it behind the building, waiting to give Tez the signal to bring it round front; but then, all the bullshit had started, so it never happened. I only saw it once the police had cleared the scene and the yellow tape had been snatched down. My truck sat behind the venue for two days before Glee took me back there. At first, I was upset that we were even back there. The memories that it had just given me hurt. We both got a surprise when we opened the truck and discovered that Tez had left me a gift on the passenger's seat. Glee insisted I opened it since he was unaware of Tez getting me anything. When I opened the card, four round trip plane tickets fell out with a note that read:

Niya a.k.a. Lil Mama witcho tough ass,

  Happy Birthday nigga! You 16 now!

I know the fam been going through it lately, but perhaps a vacation is what we need. I got all y'all asses round trip tickets to come with me and my girl to Jamaica. Since we always smokin', let's see if y'all can hang with the real rastas. The trip is for 01/01/01... we starting the year off right sis. Tell them fools get ready!

-Tez

Now that Tez was gone, we weren't even sure we wanted to go without him. As we neared his mama's block, there were cars lined down both sides of the streets. It was going to be next to impossible to find a spot. After circling the block twice and then seeing Lil drop Dasiah off in front of

Ms Teresa's house, Glee pulled up behind him and dropped me off. My sister and I watched as they both raced up the street in search of parking. After two minutes, we both headed inside to hear cheerful and funny stories about Tez.

|Glee|

The girls didn't know that today was not only the day we laid Tez to rest, but it was also the day Khalil and I would be sending Keno to meet his maker. We knew they were going to watch us up until a point and then go inside. Ms. Teresa had a big ass backyard with plenty of space for us to park, but we only needed to park Lil's whip cause he hopped in with me. We sped towards Thirty Fourth, headed towards the area where Keno's peoples told us where we could find him. All this time, Alani and Alvin was the ones in our neighborhood related to this fuck nigga. I had never paid attention to them usually being around whenever this nigga was in the vicinity. When we told Alvin that pussy had used his sister as a human shield, he agreed to help us fry this nigga. Lil was sitting in the passenger's seat, twisting the silencer on his gun.

"Hot Wheels say it's his mama house we coming to." Lil said, now concealing his weapon.

I never spoke as I navigated to the address we had been given. Alvin b.k.a Hot Wheels for his need for speed and his thrill for stealing whips had always been solid with the crew. Even though the jit was related to the opp, it didn't stop him from serving him to us on a silver platter. When we pulled up to the house across the street from the park, it was almost completely dark except for one light being on in what appeared to be the living room. I had already killed the lights and the engine as we both met at the door.

"You go round back, I'll take the front." I whispered.

Lil took off on the left side of the house. When I thought he was in position, I kicked the door in. A surprised female looked at me as Keno's dick flopped out her mouth.

"Why you sto.." He started to say. But once he opened his eyes and focused on what had her attention, he too stared at me and the barrel of my .45. His eyes were big as saucers as he snatched the girl near him, using her to block him. This fuck nigga real deal was a pussy.

"Let her go nigga!" I spat at him.

"Keno please... pleaaassseee let me go!" The girl screamed.

As if Keno was thinking about it, Khalil finally emerged from the kitchen, holding his gun and another gun. Keno's eyes grew ten times bigger as he subconsciously let the screaming girl go as he franticly stuffed his hands in the couch, presumably looking for the gun Khalil had in his hands. The girl made a run for it past me and Khalil and out the door. We weren't here to make her mama cry, but we were here to atone for the death of our fallen friend. I let

Khalil do the honors as he shot four hot bullets into Keno's body. The impact from each shot sent splatters of blood everywhere on the floral print couch. We left out the back and made our way back to my car, where we headed back across town to Tez's mom's house.

Keno had gotten caught with his pants down and only now could Tez truly rest in peace.

Chapter 10

01-01-01

|Daniya|

The traffic was crazy trying to get to Tampa, but the way that Glee drove, it was bound to take us half the time to get to the airport. Tampa International was always swamped so what made us think New Year's Day would be any different was beyond me? As traffic seemed to be on our side, we made it to the airport with plenty of enough time to get through security and have a bathroom break. This wouldn't be my first flight, but Glee had never been anywhere, especially if a car wasn't involved. We watched as Tiana and Corianna made their way over to us, and I immediately went for the bubbly eleven month old. I was so busy playing with her that hadn't noticed Lil and my sister arriving.

"I hope yo ass ain't thinking about one of those for a long ass time." My sister said, looking at Corianna laughing at the faces I was making at her.

"Nah sis, I think me and Glee gone start with a dog." I said, looking at him, trying to still campaign for the dog I had asked him for during Christmas.

"Hell you might need a dog to see how your parenting skills really are. It's more to it than silly faces." He said playfully.

As our flight to Jamaica was being called for boarding, I looked around at my traveling companions. For years to come, I hope we took more flights and achieved new shit in this new year. Tez had managed to get all the people he loved more than the streets on one adventure, and because of him, we would be having plenty of adventures in his honor. I got comfortable in my seat and grabbed Glee's hand, preparing for takeoff. I turned my CD player up and let Pac's Unconditional Love play.

♫ **"In this game, the lesson's in your eyes to see**

Though things change, the future's still inside of me

We must remember that tomorrow comes after the dark

So you will always be in my heart, with unconditional love." ♫

I was indeed unconditionally loved.

Epilogue

Fall 2005

Daniya

"I'm icy, I'm icy, I'm icy, I'm icy, I'm icy, I'm icy, I'm icy, I'm icy."

Dasiah screamed out stupid excited in my face as Tiana walked out with my birthday cake. It was equipped with sparklers, actively going off on top. Glee popped another bottle of Remy open as he tried to grab hold of our two year old daughter Shamari, who was running around with her cousins Corianna and Cortez. The last few years had brought new life for all of us. Even though Tez was no longer with us, Tiana and Corianna had gotten a more extended family with us. Corianna was now five and the spitting image of her daddy. She was the cutest thing ever and took her big cousin role serious when it came to Shamari and Cortez. Tiana had gotten close to Dasiah and I; Lil and Glee called us the three musketeers. I hustled for two and a half summers before I stopped for good. Shamari was my everything and being the perfect blend of Glee and I was the icing on top. Glee was still heavy in the streets with Khalil right by his side as they continued to build names for themselves. If you asked either of them, they was doing the shit for Tez. I smiled as Khalil came over with his and Dasiah's one and a half year old son Cortez in his grasp, and Glee had finally gotten a hold of a now upset Shamari.

"Daddy down!" She tussled in his arms.

I laughed at my daughter's feeble attempt to get out of her daddy's arms. Even on his fourth cup of Remy, Shamari was no match for him.

The pack and play was assembled and about to be utilized because it was time to blow out my candles. Once both toddlers had been secured, I stepped up to the table and paused, looking around at the very people that had gotten me through these last five years. I had grown as a woman and a mother because of them. I looked up in my man's eyes and then closed mine, making a wish over the single sheet yellow cake from Publix. The celebration of my life was small, being made up of just the eight of us. Ever since my sixteenth birthday, I had opted for smaller intimate birthdays with just me and my immediate family. This pivotal age would be no different. I watched as Khalil came up behind a very pregnant Dasiah and placed a kiss on her cheek before pulling the velvet box out of his pocket. I had gone with him a week prior to pick it out, and I was beyond elated for my sister. She deserved this moment so much, and I was glad to be here to witness it. As she turned around to him down on one knee, I watched as Khalil asked my sister to marry him. Today wasn't just my birthday. It was the day we all lost a huge part of our hearts, and if Khalil and Glee taking the time to pour out almost an entire bottle of Remy for Tez wasn't an indicator, I didn't know what else was.

All I did know was that twenty-one was looking up, and thanks to all of our guardian Angels looking out for us, we were going to make it to see another day.

--The End--